HARLEQUIN
Presents

A warm welcome to all our readers; it's cold outside, but the books Harlequin Presents has got for you in January will leave you positively glowing!

Raise your temperature with two right royal reads! *The Sheikh's Innocent Bride,* by top author Lynne Graham, whisks you away to the blazing dunes of the desert in a classic tale of a proud sheikh's desire for the young woman employed to clean his castle. Meanwhile, Robyn Donald is back with another compelling Bagaton story in *The Royal Baby Bargain,* the latest installment in her immensely popular New Zealand-based BY ROYAL COMMAND miniseries.

Want the thermostat turned up? Then why not travel with us to the glorious Greek islands, where *Bought by the Greek Tycoon,* by favorite author Jacqueline Baird, promises searing emotional scenes and nights of blistering passion, and Susan Stephens's *Virgin for Sale*—the first title in our steamy new miniseries UNCUT—sees an uptight businesswoman learning what it is to feel pleasure in the hands of a *real* man!

For Cathy Williams fans, there's a new winter warmer: in *At the Italian's Command,* the heart of a notoriously cool, workaholic tycoon is finally melted by a frumpy but feisty journalist. And try turning the pages of rising star Melanie Milburne's latest release—*Back in her Husband's Bed,* about a marriage rekindled in sunny Sydney, Australia, is *almost* too hot to handle!

For a full list of titles and book numbers, see inside the front cover (opposite)—and enjoy!

MISTRESS TO A MILLIONAIRE

*She's his in the bedroom,
but he can't buy her love...*

Showered with diamonds, draped in exquisite
lingerie, whisked around the world...

The ultimate fantasy becomes a reality.

Live the dream with more
MISTRESS TO A MILLIONAIRE titles
by your favorite authors.

Available only in Harlequin Presents®

Cathy Williams

AT THE ITALIAN'S COMMAND

MISTRESS
TO A
MILLIONAIRE

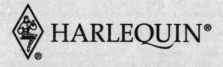

HARLEQUIN®

TORONTO • NEW YORK • LONDON
AMSTERDAM • PARIS • SYDNEY • HAMBURG
STOCKHOLM • ATHENS • TOKYO • MILAN • MADRID
PRAGUE • WARSAW • BUDAPEST • AUCKLAND

ISBN 0-373-12513-5

AT THE ITALIAN'S COMMAND

First North American Publication 2006.

Copyright © 2005 by Cathy Williams.

This edition published by arrangement with Harlequin Books S.A.

® and TM are trademarks of the publisher. Trademarks indicated with ® are registered in the United States Patent and Trademark Office, the Canadian Trade Marks Office and in other countries.

www.eHarlequin.com

Printed in U.S.A.

All about the author...
Cathy Williams

Cathy was born in the West Indies and has been writing Harlequin romances for over fifteen years. She is a great believer in the power of perseverance as she had never written anything before and from the starting point of zero has now fulfilled her ambition to pursue this most enjoyable of careers. She would encourage any would-be writer to have faith and go for it!

She loves the beautiful Warwickshire countryside where she lives with her husband and three children, Charlotte, Olivia and Emma. When not writing she is hard-pressed to find a moment's free time in between the millions of household chores, not to mention being a one-woman taxi service for her daughters' never-ending social lives.

She derives inspiration from the hot, lazy, tropical island of Trinidad (where she was born), from the peaceful countryside of middle England and, of course, from her many friends, who are a rich source of plots and are particularly garrulous when it comes to describing her heroes. It would seem from their complaints that tall, dark and charismatic men are too few and far between! Her hope is to continue writing romance fiction and providing those eternal tales of love for which, she feels, we all strive.

CHAPTER ONE

EIGHT-THIRTY on a Sunday evening. Rafe heard the phone ring next to where he was sitting, in the room that had once been a library and was now his office away from the office. Global deals had no respect for English working hours, and Sundays were never days of rest for him. They were simply time when he could catch up with whatever needed doing, make calls to Australia, make sure, in essence, that everything was ticking over nicely.

Furthermore, he knew who would be on the other end of the line.

With a little sigh of half pleasure, half frustration, he picked up the receiver and as he'd predicted heard his mother's voice on the other end of the line.

'You're working, Rafael. Aren't you? You're in that office of yours working. You shouldn't be working on a Sunday. How many times have I told you that?'

'Hullo, Mother.' He smiled into the telephone, pushed his leather chair away from the desk and swivelled round, bringing the phone with him, so that he could stare out of the window. In the depths of winter, there wasn't much to see outside, just the vague shapes of his back garden, which was large for a London house but small in comparison to the acres of land on which he had grown up. 'How are you?'

'I, Rafael, am fine. You, on the other hand, are heading for high blood pressure and an early grave.'

'Thank you for that.' He grinned and ran his fingers

through his short, dark hair. 'Never let it be said that a businessman's life isn't fraught with danger.'

He listened abstractedly as Claudia Loro continued more or less in the same vein for a few minutes, lecturing to him about his lifestyle, asking him about his health and punctuating his answers with pointed clucking and elaborate sighs. It was a familiar routine and one that he accepted with good-natured tolerance. He would never have allowed any other woman to preach to him about his life, and some had made the mistake of trying in the past, but his mother was different. He listened, even if he chose to ignore most of her advice.

She had now moved on to the topic of her week, bringing him up to date with what she had been doing, filling him in on what was happening in the little village where she lived and which had been his home until he'd moved down to London fourteen years previously. Already his mind was drifting off to Paul Glebe on the other side of the world, whose phone call had raised one or two problems that needed sorting out if his latest acquisition was to go ahead.

'Anyway,' he heard his mother say in a rounding-up tone of voice, 'I haven't called to witter on about my social life…'

'Exciting though it may be.'

'Certainly a great deal jollier than yours, my darling.'

'My life, dearest Mama, is deeply exciting.' He stretched out his long legs, resting them on the broad ledge of the window, and thought fleetingly of the current piece of excitement in his life. Five foot ten, legs up to her armpits and hair down to her waist. Intellectually undemanding but physically stunning. Just the way he liked them. What man needed a high IQ in his woman when all he wanted to do when he wasn't working was give his fiercely active brain a well-deserved rest? In short, she was just the sort of girl his mother would heartily disapprove of. He wondered whether to stoke the fire by mentioning this particular fun element of his life, and decided against it.

'But lacking in challenge, Rafael. Which is why I have a little surprise up my sleeve for you...'

The pleasant image of Angela Street and her very long legs evaporated and he grunted discouragingly, frowning at the sudden change in his mother voice. A surprise from his mother usually heralded an invitation to some informal get-together involving as many of her local friends as she could rustle up, along with their assorted offspring, in one huge, unwelcome matchmaking fest.

'I can't come,' he said bluntly. Claudia Loro ignored him.

'Do you remember Grace Frey? My very dear friend?'

'Hard not to,' Rafe said dryly. The pleasing image of his long-haired beauty was replaced by that of a woman in her late forties, small, energetic and very post-hippie.

'Then you'll surely remember her daughter. Sophie.'

Rafe all but groaned. Like her mother, Sophie Frey stuck in a person's head like a burr under the skin. She, too, was small and distinctly unfeminine. Undisciplined hair, freckles, clothes that looked as though they had been yanked out of a junk shop and then just thrown together in a random fashion with the sole objective of making their wearer as unappealing as possible. The last time he had seen her had been at his mother's summer barbecue. Sandals of the sort worn by the determined rambler, long, flowing skirt clashing horribly with a cardigan that looked as though it had been borrowed from someone's grandfather. He had studiously managed to avoid her.

'Where is this leading, Mother?'

'Straight to your office, as a matter of fact.'

While Rafe was trying to puzzle this one out, Claudia jumped into the breach to explain.

'She's just changed jobs, darling. Left that dreadful office place where she's been working and managed to land herself a job at a publishing house. Anyway, to cut a long story short, she's been thrown in at the deep end. One of their publications includes a business magazine, which isn't, I gather, doing terribly well. They're trying to revamp it into something more user friendly, which basically means incorporating more human interest stories with the usual boring financial news.'

'You're losing me here.' He swivelled back round to face his desk and brought his computer back to life with a click of a mouse. The report he had been reading before the telephone had rung was once more flickering in front of him, waiting to be checked.

'Am I, darling? And you with that sharp brain of yours?' She laughed delightedly. 'Let me explain, in that case. Sophie has to do a feature on someone big in the business world.'

'Ah.' A one-hour interview was distinctly better than an evening with the local gang. 'If she phones my secretary, I'm sure I can squeeze her in for an interview.'

'Not so much an interview, Rafael, as...' Her voice trailed off into thoughtful silence and Rafe began scrolling down the report, scanning the important points raised and already calculating what needed to be done.

'As what?' he prompted.

'As, well, something more detailed.'

'What could be more detailed than an interview? She sits in my office for half an hour, she asks questions, she writes my answers down in her little notepad, she goes away and writes her article or whatever it is she has to do. Of course, I would have to proofread anything she's written. Facts have a sinister way of becoming distorted when they're in the hands of a journalist.'

'When I say *more detailed*, darling, I mean it. Her brief is to shadow you for a fortnight, really absorb what you do and how you do it, and then write an article about the man behind the empire…'

Rafe's attention shot away from the report and focused fully on what his mother had just said.

'That's out of the question.'

'Naturally, it would be a huge scoop for their very first special feature to be about you,' Claudia Loro said calmly. 'You're wealthy, you're powerful and you lead a seemingly colourful life—'

'I said *no*, Mother, and you can relay that simple message to her.'

'She starts tomorrow. I've promised Grace that I would help Sophie out and you are not going to let me down, Rafael.'

With anyone else, Rafe Loro would have turned on that side of his personality that could make grown men quake in fear, that contemptuously cold side that brooked no argument and silenced all opposition.

Respect and love for his mother controlled the urge, but he was in no better frame of mind the following morning as he let himself into his office two hours before his secretary was due to arrive. In fact, as he settled behind his desk his mood was filthy. It wasn't often that Rafael Loro was rendered impotent and it was a sensation he didn't care for. He had no intention of resigning himself to the inevitable and making the best of it. He didn't want the girl tagging around behind him like an annoying, yapping dog and he fully intended to tell her that. If she didn't like his attitude, then she could find herself someone else to follow.

He also didn't like the idea of someone traipsing along

with him to his meetings. Did she expect him to hold her hand and make sure that she was all right? He sincerely hoped not because if she did, then her awakening to reality would be brutal. Unfortunate but inevitable.

He was still seething when the building began to come alive with people arriving at normal working hours.

Sophie, who had spent a long time working out what she should wear, was aware of his mood before she actually made it to his office.

It seemed to her that *everyone* on the director's floor was somehow tuned into the big boss's moods. His secretary, Patricia, who met her in Reception, warned her that she was in for a hard time.

'Poor you,' she said sympathetically. 'He can be pretty scary anyway, but in a bad mood he's positively terrifying. Especially when you're not used to it.'

Patricia Clark looked as though she was used to it. She was small, in her fifties, neatly attired, but under the warm expression was a glint of steel. Sophie guessed that you would need that working with someone like Rafael Loro, and she shuddered.

This was a situation she had not wanted, had not courted, but had somehow found herself steered into by their respective parents and their joint good intentions. Yes, she had certainly scored a hit with her company, but the very thought of having to be in the man's presence over a two-week period made her feel sick inside.

She glanced anxiously down at herself, wondering not for the first time whether she had worn the right clothes. Not a suit, but as close to it as she could manage without having to go out and spend her hard-earned cash on point-less clothing. Her long skirt was at least dark, as was the long-sleeved stretchy top and her coat. She had pinned back her unruly red hair as best she could, using about a thousand clips in the process, and her briefcase was small, neat and very businesslike.

'Fantastic offices,' she said politely, trying not to gape as she was led along the plushly carpeted corridor, which was buzzing on both sides with brisk-looking people. The open area was sensibly planned out, with partitions dividing certain sections, and all the furniture was of the same type—rich wood and chrome that looked wildly expensive.

Her fragile nerves took another giddy nosedive. She could picture Rafe Loro striding through this domain, *his* domain, giving orders and smiling with gratification as everyone scurried around him in a flurry of panic. At eight, she had followed him around whenever she had gone with her mother to visit their massive country house. At fourteen she had adored him from a distance, that compelling young man with his entourage of adoring friends, whom he had seemed to treat with languid amusement and a certain amount of detachment, never quite letting himself go. He had always had that kind of personality. The kind that attracted a following. Returning every holiday from his boarding-school, he had always been received like royalty by all the members of his peer group, the offspring of the rich and privileged, most of whom boarded as well before flying off to universities or finishing schools in exotic European capitals. Five years his junior, she had been in awe of him and very smitten by what she had glimpsed intermittently from a distance, because their mothers were so close to one another.

Only when he had politely told her that she was making a spectacle of herself staring at him in front of his friends, had she wised up to the fact that he really didn't like her at all. Her background was grammar-school ordinary, her house was vicarage dull, her looks were crashingly non-descript and her infatuation was comically unwelcome.

She had avoided him ever since. When she had seen him, usually at one of his mother's Christmas parties, which she was obliged to attend, she had made sure to keep out of his way. Not difficult, as Claudia Loro's parties were not small affairs.

She couldn't imagine what her mother had been thinking, getting her involved in this exercise, but then Grace had always seen him as a nice young man who had made something of himself and not rested on the laurels of that golden spoon that had been firmly wedged in his mouth the day he had been born.

She watched the busy hum of people working fade behind her as she followed Patricia towards the directors' muted, tasteful offices. The building was short and squat, interestingly fashioned around a central courtyard. The sheer size of the place made it a goodish distance to where Rafe had his office, because the directors' quarters were located on the same level but another wing.

'Brought you the long way,' Patricia was explaining. 'I thought you might be interested in seeing other sides of the company. What we left behind is the financial department.'

Sophie nodded, dazed by the opulence and dreading her destination.

Her heart was thumping by the time they finally arrived at a closed door, with a simple gilded plaque on it bearing Rafael's name.

'At least you're a family friend.' Patricia smiled. 'You'll probably lift him out of his black mood.'

Sophie considered that a seriously misguided statement. She had a sinking feeling about what had instigated the black mood in the first place, and she wasn't surprised, when she was at last ushered into his hallowed office, to be greeted with an atmosphere that could freeze fire.

'I'll take it from here, Patricia,' he said, giving a fast-quailing Sophie the full brunt of his devastating stare.

He had amazing eyes. She had always thought so. A vivid memory of being a young teenager, and fantasising about those eyes being directed at her, filled her cheeks with a bloom of uncomfortable colour. Green eyes, dramatic against his swarthy colouring and black hair. His father's eyes, because the rest of him was all his mother's Italian ancestry. The dark hair, the olive complexion, the strong, aggressive, uniquely *foreign* features.

She gathered herself quickly, although she didn't move any closer into the room, just remained where she was, hovering as the door was quietly shut behind her. Patricia had taken her coat from her and pegged it in the outside room. Without it, she felt inadequate and suddenly vulnerable under that intense, unflinching gaze.

'Sit down, Sophie,' he said finally, nodding to the chair in front of his desk.

As soon as she was sitting, he leaned forward, linking his fingers together, and spoke in a very soft, razor-sharp voice.

'I won't beat about the bush,' he told her. 'I don't want you here and the only reason you're sitting on that chair in front of this desk is because I was railroaded into it by my mother. I am an extremely busy man and I have no time to take care of someone walking in my shadow for a fortnight, but I had no choice.'

Sophie refused to shrink under those cool eyes, even though at this point she could think of nothing more enjoyable than being swallowed up by the ground.

'I realise that it's inconvenient for you, Rafe, but this whole thing was arranged without my consent either.'

He gave a short, disbelieving laugh, but let it drop.

'My schedule is intense.' He shoved a piece of paper over to her and Sophie's eyes flicked over it. A timetable that seemed to leave little room to breathe. 'You can follow me into my meetings, although I really can't see what the point of the exercise is. I work hard, but that is information I could have provided for you in the space of a five-minute meeting.' Rafe sat back and proceeded to look at her with an unreadable expression on his darkly handsome face.

Same old Sophie. Gauche, tongue-tied and dressed in the same unfortunate style as her mother. Still. He had made his position clear from the onset. He wasn't going to baby-sit her simply because of the connection between their parents.

'I already knew that you're a workaholic, Rafe—'

'I work hard. Quite different from being a workaholic.'

'I'll make a note of it.' Her blue eyes clashed with his own and he was impressed to see that her gaze was as steady as his. Must be desperate for her job, he thought. Anyone with a semblance of pride would have ditched the venture by now.

'How are you, anyway?' he asked, changing the subject, and was irritated to see that her cool expression didn't thaw even fractionally in the face of this attempt at pleasantries.

'Is that a meaningful question? I mean, are you really interested in my well-being or are you just being polite now that you've told me how you feel about my presence here?'

'I'll get back to you on that one, shall I?' He stood up, expecting her to follow suit, which she did. 'Meetings call. First one is on the other side of London with a couple of directors from a company I'm planning on buying.' He strode across to a cleverly concealed sliding walnut door, which she had barely noticed when she had entered his office, and extracted his coat, which he proceeded to shrug on. 'I move fast,' he said, briefly turning to her, 'and I don't intend to slow down so that you can catch up. If you insist on this ridiculous venture, then you either keep up or get left behind. I won't come looking for you.'

'I wouldn't expect you to.' Well, things had got off to a predictable start. He found her irritating and she disliked him. Put the two together and you were hardly going to get an easy ride, but in a way she decided that that made her job simpler. She would be able to detach herself and write a completely honest report without having to think about treading on eggshells out of consideration for him.

With that in mind, she snatched her coat from the peg in the outside office, making sure to keep on the move while she put it on, and kept pace with him, asking no questions, letting her impressions take the driving seat.

He talked, walked and reacted like a man accustomed to giving orders and having them obeyed. This came as no surprise. He had been like that even as a young teenager. She watched the reactions of other people as he strode through the offices, the way they involuntarily altered their body language in his passing presence. His towering personality radiated outwards like a forcefield, inspiring respect and possibly fear.

'Are your days normally so hectic?' she asked, once they were in the lift down.

'Where's your notepad? Shouldn't you be writing down all my answers?' The cool, velvety voice sent little prickles racing down her spine.

'That's not how I intend to handle it. I'm going to write up a report at the end of every evening and then when it's all over, I'll compile the real thing and submit it to my editor.'

'Which would be *after* you show it to me. Correct?'

'Naturally, nothing would go to print that hadn't been given the go-ahead by you.' Frankly, she hadn't really thought about that at all, and now that he had mentioned it she wondered how honest an account she would be able to give. No one liked themselves displayed, warts and all, for the world to examine. The lift juddered to a stop, they emerged and it was only when they were inside the chauffeur-driven Jaguar, that she had the chance to continue the conversation. She resolutely ploughed on in the face of him opening his briefcase and extracting a wad of papers that he clearly intended to peruse for the duration of the trip, never mind her questions.

'But I intend to write quite a detailed and frank article. Would that frighten you?'

For a second, Rafe wondered whether he had heard correctly. He snapped shut the briefcase and turned very slowly to look at her. 'Would that *frighten* me? Do I look like a man who scares easily?'

Sophie stuck her chin up, but her fingers were curled painfully around the handles of her executive briefcase. 'Everyone has their own fear zones.'

'According to…? Whom? Sophie Frey, psychologist?'

'There's no need to be sarcastic, Rafe.'

'There's every need to be sarcastic when you start trying to analyse me. You can follow me around and report factually on what you see. Wafting off into some airy-fairy land of speculation isn't going to work.'

Sophie didn't say anything and he frowned at her, fingers tapping restlessly on his leather briefcase, which was still shut.

'Nor do I intend to allow your personal feelings for me to colour whatever you write.'

'My personal feelings for you? I haven't *got* personal feelings for you! I happen to know you...no, I take that back...I happen to know who you are because our mothers have been friends for ever, but that's as far as it goes!'

'Which doesn't go a long way towards explaining that remark you made when you walked into my office this morning.'

'What remark?' There was wariness in her voice as she dredged her memory bank to try and recall what he could be talking about.

'That this business was arranged *without your consent*. Implying that you didn't want to be here any more than I wanted it. My reason is purely the nuisance factor of having you or anyone else around walking two paces behind me. What's your excuse?'

Sophie felt patches of tell-tale colour flood her cheeks. Her fingers were now gripping the briefcase so tightly that she feared they might have to be forcibly unhooked by the end of the drive. It took effort to remember that she was a grown adult, a woman of twenty-seven, who had been to art college, had had boyfriends and had worked alongside other people for the better part of three years. Those eyes on her and that powerful, sexy, charismatic face were not going to reduce her to the nervous teenager she had once been in his presence.

'My *excuse* is that I don't believe in pulling strings. Sure, I've landed a coup in kicking off this new departure for the magazine by shadowing you, but I would have preferred to have done the groundwork myself, found someone who actually might not have minded having me around for two weeks!' She glared at him.

So, he thought, the awkward mouse has teeth.

'If that's the truth, then fair enough. But whatever you write about me has to be unbiased.'

'And when you read what I've written, you have to read it with a fair eye!'

'I am a very fair man. Ask any of my employees.'

'I take it that you're giving me permission to talk to them about you?'

'Why not?'

'Because you might not like everything they have to say.'

'In which case I'll have the little beggars hung, drawn, quartered and then fed to the tigers I keep at the bottom of my garden specifically for that purpose...' He smiled slowly at her and Sophie felt her breath catch in her throat. She became acutely aware of exactly how small the back seat of a car was, even the back seat of a big car.

'I guess it's the only efficient way of dealing with detractors,' she said lightly, voice normal even though her heart was beating thunderously inside her. 'Tell me, does there ever come a time when you just feel you want to crash out? I mean, you seem to be on the go permanently.' There, much better, get the conversation back to basics.

'I enjoy what I do. Why would I want to take time out?'

'Because it's exhausting?'

'I don't tire easily.'

'Can I ask you how you got involved in your business? I mean, I know you inherited quite a bit when your father died years ago, but you've expanded...'

On firmer footing now, she could actually relax and listen to him as he gave her a potted account of his rise to his virtually untouchable status.

By the time the car was pulling up in front of a small but prestigious-looking building south of the river, she had pretty much got the factual backbone of her story mapped out in her head. A tale of a boy born into privilege, with a brain that entitled him to strive for his own goals and the burning ambition to do it. A fair bit of the story she already knew, having grown up in the same village, but it was nevertheless interesting to see his take on his situation. While he admitted to his moneyed background, it was something he obviously simply took for granted. He had never been drawn towards an excessive lifestyle, although he had not spurned the doors his family wealth had initially opened. He had taken the reins of his father's company when the time had come and from there had begun his process of branching out.

'And what will you be doing here?' Sophie asked, clambering out behind him, making sure to keep up with his long strides.

'Discussing the possibility of buying a small IT company, which I might actually hang onto for longer than usual because I think it has potential.'

'Meaning…?'

'Meaning that you are now entering a silent zone. You're to be seen and not heard. Got it?'

Any thaw in him had been brief. A salutary lesson in realising that information imparted would be solely on his terms. And the occasional smile was not an invitation to familiarity. Never had been. When she was a kid, he had viewed her as a pest. As an adult, she was far removed from his league and trawling around behind him, still a pest.

'Of course,' Sophie said neutrally.

She had planned on taking notes, but in the end was held captive by the force of his personality. A little over two hours and she felt drained by the driving energy he imparted. Points were raised and debated, columns of figures were looked at and picked over, until several of the directors were squirming in their seats. Alongside Rafe, two of his lawyers followed proceedings, interrupting when relevant but leaving the bulk of the business to be manoeuvred by him.

She wondered whether he was typical of any man in a position of power or whether this was his unique style.

Lunch turned out to be something grabbed *en route* to another meeting, and by the end of the day she felt as though she had been thoroughly put through the mill.

How on earth could anyone continue to function day after day on such high levels of adrenaline?

It was the question she put to him when, at a little after six, she was getting ready to leave. The last hour had been relatively restful, at least. She had had an opportunity to chat with Patricia and to begin writing up some of her report, escaping from him into one of the empty offices further along, which she had been allowed to use temporarily.

Rafe looked up from what he had been doing and frowned. 'I thought you'd gone. What are you still doing here?'

'I was on my way out. I was just curious to know if your energy levels ever run dry.'

'You've asked me that one already. You should take notes of what I say, then you won't run the risk of repeating yourself.'

Sophie felt like a child whose welcome had expired. She knew her image matched the feeling. Her hair had spent the day struggling to be freed from its clip-bound hell and had mostly managed to succeed. Whatever rudimentary make-up she had donned for the day had disappeared and she had done nothing to replenish her lipstick, which meant that that too would have vanished. Her clothes, at least, had been functional given the nature of her day, but she had been all too conscious of their lack of appropriateness. In fact, at two of the meetings, several of the younger men had looked at her curiously, as though bemused by her oddity. Rafe, in all fairness, had said nothing, but she knew that he was thinking the same. And now it was time for her to leave.

'I'm sorry. I didn't realise how packed your timetable is. The reality just seems a lot more driven than some entries made on a sheet of paper.'

'Like I said, I won't be slowing my pace to accommodate you.'

'And as *I've* said, I won't be expecting it.' She hovered irresolutely by the door, wondering how to take her line of questioning one step further without it backfiring onto her.

Watching her, Rafe sat back and folded his hands behind his head. She had proved less of an irritation to him during the course of the day than he had expected, but then again she had, apart from that fleeting conversation in the car, spoken very little. He assumed she had watched him, but most of the time he had forgotten her presence altogether.

She was beginning to irritate him now, however, because he could sense her eagerness to discover something more personal about him, more than just the nuts and bolts of how someone ran an empire. That sort of information was predictably easy to acquire. It usually boiled down to hard work and gritty determination in the face of possible set-backs.

But if she was fired up with a mission to get to a personal level, nuts and bolts of company running wasn't going to be enough. He allowed her to squirm for a few more moments.

'If you're finished for the day, then I would really like to get back to work,' Rafe said politely, masking his distaste behind a veneer of politeness. 'Unless, of course, you want to watch me pouring over these reports in silence.'

'No.' Sophie flashed him an awkward smile. 'Shall I come here at the same time tomorrow morning?'

'You can if you want to, but I won't be here.' He flicked through a palm-held device. 'I have a breakfast meeting at seven at the airport with some international bankers. More of the same as today, I'm afraid. Maybe you could utilise your time more efficiently by having a look at the company from the inside. I'll tell Patricia to show you around.'

'Oh, right. Yes. That sounds a good idea.'

'Fine.' On that note, he sat forward and devoted his attention to the papers in front of him. He was aware of her presence, still hovering like a spectre by the door. 'Run along now, Sophie,' he said, flicking her a brief glance. 'I have a lot to get through before I go out tonight.'

'More clients?'

Rafe made a point of looking at his watch. 'And the time is…nearly six-thirty. I would say your day of shadowing is resoundingly at an end, wouldn't you?'

'I was just trying to formulate a picture in my head of someone whose work life never ceases. I know you probably think that I'm being nosy, but for me to get a complete picture—'

'You mean as opposed to the one-dimensional cardboard cut-out one you're currently nurturing? Workaholic with an addiction to money-making?' Rafe sat back and gave her a long, lazy look. 'Well, sorry to blow your preconceived notions, but no clients tonight. Would you like to come along and sit in on my dinner date? See how the power-obsessed tycoon enjoys his leisure time?'

He was actually smiling with satisfaction at her discomfort when she shut the door behind her.

Poor little Sophie. Might have been a bit different if he hadn't known her from way back when, if he didn't still see her as the awkward kid who had never been able to say boo to a goose. She was a bit more sparky now than he remembered, but it was hard to drop the preconceived impressions. With a little shrug, he returned to his papers and within five minutes any thoughts of Sophie Frey had been completely forgotten.

CHAPTER TWO

WINTER, as always, was living down to expectations. No one living in London reasonably expected snow, although it might have been nice, but neither did they expect a relentless deluge of freezing rain.

Rafe, more or less inured against the vagaries of bad weather thanks to the convenience of having his own private chauffeur, was absent-mindedly contemplating those less fortunate outside when he picked out a familiar figure struggling along the pavement, head downturned, hands stuck into the pockets of her coat.

For a few seconds he toyed with the idea of pretending that he hadn't seen her, then with an impatient sigh he instructed his chauffeur to pull over to the kerb.

Sophie, bracing herself against the rain and wishing to God that she had had the sense to travel with her umbrella, almost crashed into the open car door before she realised that it was there.

'Get in, Sophie.' Rafe leaned across the seat and suppressed another little twinge of annoyance as she bent down and peered into the back seat. 'What the hell are you doing out without an umbrella?'

'Making my way home,' Sophie retorted. 'Along with the rest of London.'

'Well, you might as well climb in.' He drew back and was aware of her dripping her way into the back seat of the car.

'I'm sorry. I'm soaking wet. Are you sure it's all right?

I mean, I wouldn't want to damage the upholstery of your car.'

'Close the door behind you. You're letting the rain in.'

Sophie slammed the door shut with a feeling of exquisite relief. Anything to be out of that driving cold rain. She shrugged out of her coat, trying to ignore the cool green eyes on her, and then stuffed it on the floor well at her feet.

'Thank you.' She turned to him and tried a pleasant smile on for size. 'I didn't realise that you'd come back to the office. Patricia said that you would probably go straight home from your last meeting.'

'One or two things to do.' The rain had dampened down the curls and turned the copper-red colour to an odd sort of brown. Her face, devoid of make-up, was pale and damp. He wondered whether she ever looked in a mirror at all. 'Where are you staying?'

Sophie gave him the address, which was on the outskirts of London, and Rafe frowned.

'I haven't got time to drop you there. You'll have to drop me off first and then George will take you to where you live.'

Sophie opened her mouth to argue the point and then nodded her head. She had to get out of the habit of feeling awkward in Rafe's presence, at least if she were to do her job with any level of competency. She had to will herself to talk to him so that she could find out what made him tick. He treated her like a kid because his mind was stuck in that groove, but that gambit only worked if she allowed herself to be treated that way.

'That's fine,' she said coolly. 'Did you have a productive day?'

'The forecast is good on several fronts,' Rafe said, sitting back and leaning against the door so that he could watch her more thoroughly. 'What about you? Did you manage to make the rounds of the office and get hold of any juicy titbits about me?'

'It seems you're the perfect boss, Rafe. No one had a bad word to say about you, but then I don't suppose they would have felt inclined to pour their hearts out to a virtual stranger.'

'So, disappointment on that front, then.'

'I admit my editor might have enjoyed some gossip,' Sophie told him truthfully, 'but it seems that you pay well and treat your employees fairly. Group meetings on a regular basis so that they can let off steam, pay reviews bi-annually, membership of a sports centre, bonus packages at the end of the year, the list goes on.'

'What did you expect, Sophie? A tyrant who chained his workers to their desks and deprived them of everything but the basics?'

'Of course not! But I've worked in an office. I know that there are always grumblings of discontent around if you look hard enough.'

'Is that why you left your job? Because of the office politics?' He realised that, although they had met socially off and on over the years, he knew very little about her. She had stuck in his head as someone who hovered on the sidelines, always standing out like a sore thumb but not for the right reasons. 'You did a degree in Art,' he remarked, remembering one piece of throwaway information his mother had given him at some point. He recalled thinking that that was exactly what he would have guessed she might have done, given her appearance.

'How do you know that?'

'My mother must have told me at some point. Why the jump from art to office work?'

'Because finding a job that involved my art degree was impossible,' Sophie informed him shortly. 'Why do you think you weren't content on simply taking over your father's business? It was extremely profitable. Why did you feel compelled to expand it to the extent that you have?'

Rafe recognised the ploy. She was uncomfortable talking about herself and so made her answers as brief and monosyllabic as possible before changing the subject. He couldn't blame her. When had he ever shown the slightest interest in her? But since they were cooped up with one another for two weeks, what normal human being wouldn't show some level of interest?

'Ah. The fascinating question of motivation,' Rafe drawled. 'What do *you* think?'

'I can't write an article on what *I* think about you. I have to write an article based on what I observe and what you tell me about yourself.'

'No one likes to rest on inherited wealth. I branched out because I had to flex my own intellectual muscles.'

It was an answer within a non-answer. Yes, it provided facts in a nutshell, but that fascinating question of motivation that he had mentioned earlier remained unanswered. And Sophie got the feeling that he was all too aware of the fact and was not about to do anything about it. He was very private and any excavating of his character, which really was what her editor would want to see, would have to be done very carefully.

She would have to make him feel relaxed in her company and maybe then he might let slip the odd remark that would reveal something about himself.

It helped that he saw her as nothing more than an irritating kid who had grown up. Despite any surface interest he expressed in her and what she had been doing with her life, he honestly didn't care.

She tried not to feel vaguely hurt and insulted by that. In a way, she almost preferred the dismissive hint of impatience, the glancing look that barely took her in, to the look he was giving her now. Green eyes coolly detached, as though she just happened to be something sexless and characterless that had happened to stray within his line of vision, thereby forcing him to react in one way or another.

In this case, pretending to show an interest in what she thought. Sophie decided that she didn't much care. The object of the exercise was to get him to open up.

'Well, it's always good to set challenges for yourself,' Sophie she said, hoping her voice had attained the right level of cosiness and warmth. 'Actually, that's what I told myself when I ended up working in an office.'

Rafe's voice was polite and only mildly interested. 'That your dreams of being the next Picasso were nothing compared to the challenges of mastering the filing system and coming to grips with PowerPoint?'

His wryly sarcastic response immediately had her hackles up. 'Actually, I never had dreams of being the next Picasso. My degree wasn't in fine art. I studied graphic design and illustration.'

'And I take it the office where you worked had no available department that could make use of your skills?'

Sophie smiled reluctantly. 'Not many legal offices do, although I did acquire a very sound knowledge of the basics of family law.'

Her face changed when she smiled. There was something graceful and cautious and very appealing about it.

'We'll be at my place in five minutes,' he said abruptly. 'I recommend you come inside and get into something dry. I don't want the responsibility of sending you home in soaking wet clothes so that you can come down with pneumonia.'

'In that case, I'll take the responsibility away from you by telling you that I'm fine to make my way home and change when I get there. In case you haven't noticed, I don't usually walk around with a spare set of clothes in my handbag.'

Rafe wasn't sure whether to be irritated or amused by her. She certainly wasn't the silent little thing he had expected. On the other hand, he was in a hell of a rush and in no mood to listen to someone trying to have a meaningful conversation with him on the subject of life choices.

'We're here.' The car had pulled up outside an exquisite mews town house, and Rafe was already pushing open his door. 'I don't intend to have a debate on the subject. I have spare clothes that my mother leaves from time to time when she visits. Granted, they may not be the height of youthful style, but I'd say you would be better off in them than enduring another forty minutes in soaking splendour. I'm due out this evening, and I'm running late. George can drop me off to the theatre and then take you home. Make your choice.'

Common sense won over pride. She felt hideously uncomfortable. Her clothes were sticking to her like a layer of ice-cold cling film and Lord only knew what was happening to her coat on the ground by her feet. Probably developing a nice coating of mildew even as he spoke.

'Thank you very much,' Sophie said, quickly shifting out of the car while he strode ahead of her. The driving rain had become a fine, sharp drizzle and she flung her coat loosely over her as she ran to keep pace with him.

George, with whom Rafe clearly had a close rapport, took himself off in the direction of what she supposed was the kitchen and she was left dripping in the hallway.

'Follow me,' Rafe commanded, barely bothering to look around.

It hardly gave Sophie a chance to appreciate her surroundings, but what she glimpsed as she raced behind him was impressive and a little surprising. She had expected chrome and wood and the expensive furnishings of a bachelor living in the fast lane. Lots of leather everywhere, perhaps, and abstract paintings on the walls. Instead, she was surprised to see that his house was warm and lived in, without a hint of chrome anywhere. The floor was wood, certainly, but deep, rich wood with the patina of time showing in it.

She would have liked to have had a look around some of the rooms, but he had already reached a bedroom that his mother obviously used when she visited.

'Clothes,' he said, opening a wardrobe. 'More in the drawers. Bathroom just there.' He nodded to an *en suite* bathroom. 'You'll need to be ready in half an hour if I'm to make this appointment in time. And leave your clothes. I'll get Anya to take care of them tomorrow when she comes.'

'Anya?'

'My housekeeper.' He paused and gave her a quick once-over. 'You didn't really think that I looked after this place without help, did you?'

'I didn't really give it much thought at all,' Sophie returned without batting an eye. 'I'll be quick.'

She was. Hardly any time to luxuriate in the bath, and it was a bathroom made for luxuriating. The bath was deep and someone had stocked up on some delightful miniature soaps and bottles of fragrant bath foam. Claudia, she suspected. Those little touches spoke of a woman and if she spent time regularly in London with her son, then she would have provided that feminine attention to detail that he would never have considered.

Unless, of course, some other woman had seen fit to domesticate the house.

Sophie dried quickly, her mind playing on that possibility. Her editor wanted human interest and that would be very interesting indeed. He was photographed often enough with some woman adorning his arm, not one but a succession of them. Small soaps in a glass jar and that porcelain jar of pot pourri spoke of someone a little more permanent than a passing notch on the bedpost.

And he would have no problem finding any woman he wanted, she thought, dressing quickly in the first thing she could find. He had the sex-appeal syndrome in buckets.

She thought back to the times she had seen him at his mother's house or wandering through the town on an exeat or during the holidays. Even from the innocent perspective of a young teenager, she had been struck by his popularity with the opposite sex. In fact, they had danced attendance upon him. And the years had been unnaturally kind to him. He still had the athletic build, but now there was something more powerful about it, and his aggressive personality showed on his face. She, personally, found it off-putting, but not many women would.

From the half a dozen or so outfits, she picked something the least formal. A straight brown skirt, a blouse, a camel-coloured cashmere jumper. Any attempt to do something neat with her hair, she abandoned completely, leaving it to curl disastrously around her face and down her back. The overall effect wasn't too much of a catastrophe, and she was on time. In fact, early.

Rafe got to the top of the stairs and paused, a little startled by the transformation.

'Early,' he said, descending the staircase and knotting his bow-tie at the same time. 'Not a trait I've often found in a woman.'

Sophie swung round at the sound of his voice and watched him as he walked slowly down towards her. She opened her mouth to say something and nothing came out. Her throat felt dry and her stomach was doing funny things too. Weird little somersaults.

The logical voice in her head was telling her that, yes, he did look stunningly handsome. White shirt, black trousers, black bow-tie, black jacket, which he was casually slinging on as he descended the staircase. Her body, on the other hand, was reacting as though she were seeing him for the first time.

'I'll go and get George,' Rafe said. 'Don't move. I'll be back in two minutes.'

Move? Sophie wondered whether her legs were capable of managing that perfectly normal function.

It was only as he disappeared from the hallway that her common sense finally kicked in, and with a vengeance. If she couldn't control some pathetic response to his masculinity, then she would have no choice but to admit defeat and hand the job over to someone else. The thought was tempting, but running away from the challenge of her first assignment would be signing her own death warrant as far as Noma Publishing was concerned, and she wanted the job. Badly.

It wasn't, she thought feverishly, as though she even *liked* the man. The visible package was good, but the contents left her cold.

With that lodged firmly at the forefront of her mind, she was functioning a bit more normally when he appeared with George in tow.

Her voice sounded steady as she slipped into the passenger seat and asked him normal, polite questions about what he was going to see and whether, for him, the outing would be rated as business or pleasure. All the time, she had to stop herself from staring. In the dark back seat of the car, his lean face was all shadows and angles. She managed to contort herself so that she was physically as far away from him as possible, but she was still aware of the tiny distance that separated their knees from touching. If it weren't so pathetic, she knew it would have been laughable.

'Sometimes the lines between business and pleasure overlap,' he was saying, his deep, velvety voice perfectly cool and controlled. 'The play will be good, I'm sure, and the networking will be invaluable.'

'And, of course, that's the main thing, isn't it?' Sophie remarked more acidly than she had meant. He was quick to pick up on the intonation in her voice.

'It's how big business works, Sophie. Does that surprise you? Maybe you disapprove of the fact that client dinners and trips to the theatre are all methods of oiling the wheels. When I'm being entertained by people, I'm almost always aware that there's a subtext, that the expensive restaurants are ways of making sure that I keep them in mind should I ever find myself in a position where I can do them a favour.'

'And that doesn't bother you?'

'Why should it? On a smaller scale, it happens every day to all of us.'

'I don't make it a habit of buttering people up just in case I might find them useful at a later date.'

'How heroic of you.'

'There's nothing heroic about it. I just don't like the thought of using people.'

'You mean,' Rafe said thoughtfully, 'you're yourself whatever the situation...' He looked at her earnest face and the cloud of wildly spiralling hair framing it and felt a surprising kick of interest. Her soft lips were drawn together in a tight line and disapproval radiated from her in waves. Not many women disapproved of him, he realised suddenly. In fact, most tripped over themselves to make sure that he noticed them in all the right ways. It made a change to be confronted with someone who didn't slot easily into the box. Especially, he thought, since it was a temporary situation.

'I like to think so.'

'And if I told you that I don't like women arguing with me, unless it's in the boardroom, you wouldn't edit your reactions at all? Not even if your assignment hung in the balance…?'

'Are you saying that I have to agree with everything you say or else you refuse to let me shadow you?' Anger bubbled in her and spilled over. 'Is that some kind of threat? I think it's very sad if you feel that you have to surround yourself with yes-people! Or maybe you're just talking about the opposite sex! Is that it? You like women to be seen and not heard and if they're heard, it's only on the condition that they saying something to flatter you!' She found that she was leaning towards him, trembling.

Looking at her, Rafe was torn between bursting out laughing and carrying on with his infuriating line of chauvinistic arrogance just to see how far he could go. There was something infinitely invigorating about her reaction. Whether she realised it or not, it was, in fact, proof that she refused to toe the line.

She also looked quite pretty, all worked up like that. Her cheeks were flushed and that riotous hair gave her the look of an angry child.

'It was a hypothetical question,' Rafe said, raising his eyebrows in amusement. 'Of course I don't surround myself with yes-people.'

'But I bet you don't have too many women disagree with what you say,' Sophie shrewdly flung back at him. 'Forgetting the ones you meet in the boardroom.' She sat back, a delayed reaction to the fact that she was much too close to him for comfort. He had been winding her up, she could see that now. It was infuriating. How could she do her job properly if he didn't even take her seriously? What Claudia and her mother had seen as an advantage, the fact that he wasn't a stranger to her, was conversely actually working against her.

'I'm not generally disagreeable when I'm in the company of a woman,' Rafe drawled. His eyes followed the movements of her hands as they gathered her hair behind her, twisting it into a makeshift pony-tail. No good. As soon as she released the tousled mass, it tumbled back around her. For someone who had not a streak of vanity in her, or so it seemed, he wondered why she hadn't long ago had the lot chopped off. But maybe—he toyed with the tantalising idea—his one-dimensional idea of her wasn't quite as accurate as he had imagined.

'But then again,' he mused, his eyes still lingering on her face, 'they don't usually set out to have arguments.'

'I wasn't *arguing* with you,' Sophie said stubbornly. 'I was voicing my opinions.'

'Ah, yes. Fine distinction.' With regret, he saw the theatre lit up ahead of them. 'An argumentative woman is only one step away from being a shrew and not many men like a shrew.'

Sophie's mouth fell open. She decided that she wasn't going to be caught again by him having a laugh at her expense. 'I'll bear that in mind,' she said tartly. 'Now, about tomorrow. What time would you like me to be there? Patricia's printed off a list of your meetings over the next few days and I see that you have your first meeting in High Wycombe at nine-thirty. Shall I meet you there or would you like me to come to the office first?'

'That's a sensitive meeting.' Rafe frowned. It occurred

to him that he hadn't given old Mr Beardsman a thought for some time.

'What do you mean by sensitive?'

'It means that I don't want you around.' The car pulled up gently to the kerb, which was teeming with people. The rain had subsided, but even so most of them carried umbrellas just in case, or else were wearing coats with hoods.

He began opening the door and she reached out and laid her hand on his arm. 'Why not?'

'Because…' Rafe shook his head in exasperation. 'Oh, for God's sake, Sophie. Why don't you do something useful? Have tea with my mother and the pair of you can talk about me till the cows come home.'

'Why don't you want me at this meeting? Is there something *illegal* going on?'

Rafe's mouth twitched with unconcealed amusement. 'Yes,' he said gravely, 'it's all highly illegal goings-on and I don't want you there in case you blow my cover.'

'Very funny, Rafe. Why can't you try and treat me like an adult?'

'Okay. Meet me there at nine-fifteen. I'll make my own way there and get George to collect you from your house. Satisfied?'

'Very. Thank you.' She sat back and gave him a smug smile. 'Have a nice evening.'

She felt curiously alive for the remainder of the evening. The project was going well, she told herself, hence her high spirits. The image of Rafe, dressed to kill, floated in her head and she squashed the picture hurriedly. He wasn't a *man* to her, he was an object of an exercise.

Still, she took care dressing the following morning. Instead of her normal attire of flowing skirt and jumper, she wore a pair of grey trousers and a slim-fitting woollen grey top with little pearl buttons halfway down the front, something she had worn a couple of times to functions at her previous office. As an afterthought, she did away with the assortment of useless clips and instead braided her hair into a French plait. Not quite as neat, but less severe than scraping the lot back and at least escaping tendrils wouldn't look so inappropriate.

With her briefcase and her now dry coat, she arrived at the small, shabby building feeling the epitome of the career girl.

Her mother, she thought, would be startled and a little taken aback at the image. Grace had always wanted her daughter to work, somehow, in the field of art. Granted, the publishing job met with slightly more favour than the office one had, but anything that essentially lacked creativity would be a disappointing waste of her daughter's talent as far as she was concerned.

Sophie resolved to live up to her image and make sure that there were no emotional outbursts of any kind. Hence the brisk smile on her face as she greeted Rafe, who nodded curtly at her. Next to him was an elderly man, short, plump, with anxious, kindly eyes and a shiny grey suit that looked clean but old. The small front room was empty and, with the exception of a young girl behind a desk manning two phones, there was no sign of activity anywhere. Not a place she would have associated with the thrusting Rafael Loro, although he looked not in the slightest ill at ease with his surroundings. If anything, he seemed impatient to be off, quickly introducing her and then cutting short pleasantries by glancing at his watch.

'I want to get this wrapped up as soon as possible, Bob,' he said, practically herding them towards a door at the side of the room. 'We've chatted enough times and now I want your answer.'

Sophie trailed behind them, watching their body language from behind. The old man's somehow defeated, Rafe's eloquent of that restless energy that could be so unnerving.

'It's a big decision, Mr Loro,' Bob said as soon as the door was closed behind them. He wiped his forehead with his handkerchief and rested both arms on the table separating them. Sitting just behind him, she couldn't see the expression on his face, but from his voice she could tell that whatever transaction was being completed was not to the old man's liking.

'It's not really that big, Bob.' Rafe's voice implied that he had gone over this ground many times before. 'Your company is on the rocks without hope of salvation. You owe people left, right and centre. You have had to lay off the majority of your staff and those who remain do so without any certainty of payment. I am offering to take all those cares off your hands.'

'It's a family company, Mr Loro! My grandfather built this up from scratch.'

'And would hate to have seen it in the hands of receivers, who can be very impersonal when they do their job.'

And so it went on over a painful hour and a half. Rafe, brutally realistic and determined, the old man looking for ways of making the sale less unpalatable.

Eventually, Rafe looked at his watch and stood up. No handshake this time. He merely looked dispassionately at Bob and said in a low, level voice, 'We've run out of talk now. You either sell or you don't, and I'm giving you precisely one week to put my offer to your family. If you agree, then I will fix up all the necessary meetings with lawyers. If you don't…' He shrugged, heading for the door. 'The world is full of sharks and if you think that I am one of them, then let me tell you that there are many with far sharper teeth.'

'How *could* you?' Sophie accused as soon as they were once more in the car. George had stayed on the premises, obviously warned in advance that their meeting would not be an all-day event.

'How could I what?' Rafe's voice was cold and silky.

'That poor old man. He was utterly intimidated by you!'

'You're shadowing me, Sophie, not offering comments on how I run my business. My advice to you is to stick to what you know.'

'I know basic decency!'

'You know nothing,' Rafe intoned coldly. He turned to her as soon as they were in the car. 'Life isn't about living in a cosy little cocoon. It's about being one step ahead of the game. Take notes, Sophie, because this bit's important. I'm where I am today because I stay ahead of the game. It's not a crime and it's not a sin, it's just life.'

'You mean you stay ahead of the game at the expense of other people!'

Rafe looked at her flushed face through narrowed eyes. Just about now, he should shrug and let her stew in her own blinkered misconceptions. After all, since when did he ever feel compelled to justify his behaviour to anyone? His mother, yes, perhaps, but even she knew that what he did in business was not her concern.

'I'm saving Bob from a worse fate,' he said finally. 'His company has made furniture for decades and with each passing year the demand for expensive handmade furniture has become less and less. It can't compete with the cheap imitations and that's just a fact of life, whether you like it or not. So here's the simple equation for you—either Bob sells to me, and my offer is about the most generous he'll get, or he goes under, sees every small asset whipped away from under him and finds himself liable for his outstanding debts, which are not inconsiderable. There is no way he can sell the company as a going concern.'

'Then why are you so interested in buying it?'

Rafe sighed irritably. 'Why are you so interested in the outcome of a deal you will have long left behind you in a few days' time?'

'Because it's a reflection of you!' Sophie told him. 'Which,' she made sure to add quickly, 'is what I'm here for. To find out about *you*.' Her blue eyes tangled with his green ones and something inside her stirred uneasily. Was that the whole truth? The question fluttered inside her, just a shadowy thought that gently tugged at the foundations, nothing alarming, just...

She gave him a bright, conciliatory smile. 'Hence the nosiness. I know you don't like it, but you could say that it's my job...'

'Okay. Here's a question for you, in that case—what did you notice about the building?'

Sophie frowned in puzzlement. 'It seemed a little tired and very quiet...'

'And also sitting in quite a bit of derelict land, wouldn't you agree?'

'You're buying that poor man's family business because of the *land*?'

Rafe flushed, annoyed with himself for offering an explanation that was essentially none of her business. What had possessed him? The girl was like a damned dog with a bone, a small, energetic, questioning and highly irritating dog. Furthermore that horrified, accusatory look in her eyes was getting on his nerves.

'What exactly is your problem here?'

'What are you going to do with the land? It's in the middle of nowhere!'

'I am going to sit on it for a while and then I intend to turn the place into an out-of-town shopping village.'

'Right, so let me get this straight. That poor old man, who has probably spent his whole life working for his family business, is going to have the lot demolished by a greedy tycoon who wants to make a quick buck by building lots of unsightly shops!'

Rafe's lips thinned with outrage. 'No one speaks to me like that!' His voice was like the crack of a whip, which Sophie steadfastly ignored. As she ignored, too, the forbidding expression on his face.

'Is making money the only thing that motivates you?'

'It's the only thing that motivates the vast majority of the human race,' Rafe growled, flushing darkly. 'Deny it if you can.'

'It's not the *only* thing that motivates. There are other things in life as well! Having fun, for one!'

'What did you do last night?'

'Last night?' Distracted, Sophie frowned. 'Nothing, why?'

'Night before?'

'I think I watched some telly.'

'What are you doing tonight?'

'I get where you're heading, Rafe! But at least my whole life doesn't revolve around work!'

'Nor does mine. In fact, it's purely about fun. Dinner with friends at Romano's in Fulham tomorrow night. Why don't you join us? After all, you do want to get the *complete* picture, don't you? Unless you're busy? Unless someone important in your life you're currently having fun with is taking you out?'

Sophie scowled at him and he shot her a glance of lazy amusement.

'Well? Prepared to take up the challenge? In your quest to find out all about me, which is the point of the exercise…?'

'Just tell me what time!'

CHAPTER THREE

PROVOKED into agreeing to join Rafe and friends for dinner, Sophie had found herself the following lunchtime taking time out to do something she very rarely did, namely clothes shopping.

Having grown up with a mother who had drummed into her from an early age that a fancy dress did not 'maketh' the girl, Sophie had spent her teenage years good-naturedly following her friends into shops, watching as they had tried on various outfits, which they had generally had little intention of buying, and resisting their persuasions to go down the same route.

'I don't honestly see the point,' she had said on several occasions. 'I'm comfortable in what I wear.' It had become a mantra so deeply ingrained that she had never felt as though she stood out in her teenage crowd, even though she had. Now, older, she still refused to give in to the passing trends, some of which were ridiculous and uncomfortable, but she was very much aware that, in so doing, she set herself apart from the mainstream crowd of young twenty-somethings who flaunted as much as they could get away with just so long as they attracted attention.

Attracting attention had never been high on her agenda of must-do's.

She had never had too much trouble making friends and having boyfriends and she had proudly told herself that her unwillingness to go with the fashion flow was a mark of her strength of character.

Until now.

Rafe's jibe at her lack of social life was all wrapped up with the way he looked at her, the way his eyes skirted over her, dismissing her as a woman. Of course, that in itself didn't matter, but still…it rankled.

Bad motive for clothes shopping, she thought now, gazing down at what she had impulsively bought five hours previously.

Turquoise was a very daring colour, especially considering they were in the depths of winter, although at the time Sophie had been persuaded by the salesgirl into thinking that it was *vibrant*. The description had appealed because it was the one word she would never have used to describe herself and the one thing she wanted to convey to Rafael Loro, arrogant, patronising bastard that he was.

So here I am now, she thought glumly, *the proud possessor of a skin-tight turquoise dress in suspicious stretch material.* She held it up by the tips of two fingers and glanced into the shoebox where a pair of high-heeled shoes were waiting to put in their appearance. Her fantasies of wiping that smug smile off Rafe's face now seemed absurd. Who cared if he spent every second of the remainder of her assignment smiling smugly?

Before she had left the office, he had given her precise directions to the restaurant, as if he somehow didn't trust her to have sufficient wit to communicate her destination to a cab driver. He had also, as an afterthought, informed her that she could bring along a *companion* if she liked. She would have to have been blind not to have seen the shadow of a snigger that had accompanied his apparently well-intentioned remark.

She decided to wear the overpriced turquoise nonsense she had bought, and very nearly managed to convince herself that she would feel good in it.

An hour and a half later she stared back at her reflection with a sinking heart.

She was no longer looking at Sophie Frey. Sophie Frey, of the comfortable, baggy clothes and no make-up, had gone into hiding. Here was someone else. Red hair tumbled down in riotous curls, mascara and eye liner emphasised huge blue eyes, and a figure normally scrupulously hidden away now flaunted curves that Sophie was only dimly aware of possessing. The shoes made her legs look longer and thinner than they possibly could be.

She decided that it was a blessing that she would not be having to conduct any sensible, work-oriented conversations because she certainly didn't feel very sensible in what she was wearing.

Her parents had been wrong, she thought as she sat in the back seat of the taxi, clutching her impractical black purse. There was a lot to be said for uncomfortable clothes. They made no sense on an everyday basis, but, as a one-off, they certainly did some weird personality-altering things. She felt *sexy*!

The restaurant, where she was eventually deposited fifteen minutes late, was tucked away and cleverly pretending to be a house. Only a discreet sign heralded that it was a restaurant at all.

Sophie felt a slight flutter of panic as she entered. Then the manager removed her coat and scarf, and sexy Sophie was back in place, smiling confidently as she was shown to Rafe's table.

She could not remember a time when conversation had stopped for her. At school, she had always been the girl next door, never a threat to any of her girlfriends, never one of those girls sought after by the boys because they promised things with their eyes and the way they moved. She had never minded. In fact, she had come to see that, as spectator sports went, watching the world go by was a pretty good one. Later, out of her teens, she had had boy-friends and they had been nice guys, the sort you could always introduce to the parents and know that they would like him as much as you did.

As she approached the full table she now felt like *one of those girls* and it was crazy, but she enjoyed the feeling.

Not knowing anyone there, she inadvertently sought out Rafe. Her heart thudded for the space of a couple of sec-onds as his green, shuttered eyes caught hers, then the si-lence was broken with a series of introductions.

'You're late,' Rafe said as soon as she was seated next to him. 'I thought you were one of those women who al-ways ran to time…'

'Blame the taxi driver,' Sophie lied, lifting her wineglass to her lips and not quite meeting his eyes. In the daze of introductions, she had not only noticed how magnificent he looked, but had also taken in the cool blonde seated on the other side of him. Angela Street had not been introduced as a girlfriend, but she certainly fitted the description. Long, blonde, blue-eyed and leaning possessively into him, arm touching arm, her low silk top gaping just enough to pro-vide him with a teasing promise of what lay in store for later that night.

'Maybe he was in temporary shock at seeing you in that very…what is the word I'm looking for?…*racy* little num-ber…' Rafe allowed his eyes to drift downwards in purely masculine appreciation. When she had walked in, he had done a double take. Had it been his imagination or had the entire table fallen silent? He, certainly, had been rendered momentarily speechless at the sight of her. Speechless and a little taken aback, because the last thing he had been expecting had been a siren in a dress that looked as though it had been spray-painted on.

'He didn't actually see the *racy* little number, as I was wearing a very thick, very old-fashioned black coat.' Rafe had turned his back on the blonde and, out of the corner of her eye, Sophie could see the curtain of white hair falling forward as Angela attempted to regain his attention.

'I think your girlfriend wants you,' Sophie informed him politely.

For a brief moment, Rafe felt a spurt of irritation as Angela's hand covered his thigh, her long fingers stroking him through the fine wool of his trousers. Two months ago, it would have aroused him. Now, he shifted his body weight slightly, just enough for her to remove her hand.

'I would never have guessed that you owned anything so…small,' Rafe said, watching Sophie as he swigged back the remaining wine in his glass. 'What's happened to the swirling skirts and grandad cardigans?'

Sophie flushed, fully aware that every time he had seen her she had been sensibly dressed, nothing impractical, nothing that made walking uncomfortable.

'I decided to give them a rest,' she said coolly. 'If you don't talk to your girlfriend pretty soon, I think she's going to have an apoplectic fit.' Turning her back on him, and with her cheeks still burning from his jibe, Sophie let herself fall in with the general conversation going on around her.

The chat was general, and within a few minutes she was aware of the dynamics of the assembled party. Paul and Emily Hass were university friends, and it said a lot about Rafe that he still communicated with people from so many years back. It was easy for him to see the people he had grown up with, since their parents still lived in the same town as his and the annual get-togethers would always be a source of catching up. Sophie had been to sufficient of those parties to have seen it in action. The girls who had become wives and then mothers, still flirting with Rafe while their husbands weren't looking, and the boys who had grown into men and gradually given in to the curse of thinning hair and paunches. As a relative outsider to the privileged, golden group, and years younger, she had been happy to watch from the sidelines and mingle with the old-ies.

For him to have kept in touch with friends from university would have required effort, and she rethought her assumption that effort was the one thing he did not expend on the human race.

Joe Marciano and his wife, Florence, both in their forties, were business friends. They were affable, affluent and very keen to discuss the vagaries of the property market, the headaches of having two teenage children and their plans to move abroad at some point. It was a congenial mix.

And helping things along was Adrian Walsh, who was seated to the right of her. His attention was flattering and convenient because it gave her an opportunity to distance herself from Rafe. When he asked her where she had been hiding all these years when surely she must have known that he was out there, looking for her, Sophie couldn't help giggling.

'I've been hiding away in a dusty lawyer's office, running errands.' She smiled, half concentrating on being charmed and half concentrating, against her will, on Rafe, who was holding the rest of his audience captive with an amusing anecdote about one of his deals that had flopped.

'And before then?'

'Art college.'

'You paint?'

Sophie toyed with her food and gave him the usual re-hearsed speech about illustrative art and how it differed from fine art. She was aware of Angela murmuring something to Rafe and his low laughter, and for a second her stomach twisted into a painful knot.

'Shame,' Adrian was saying. 'I've always wanted to have my portrait commissioned.'

'Which would be a very vain thing to do,' Sophie scolded, pleased when he laughed out loud at her reprimand. They were playing a light-hearted game of flirting, which was something she had never done before, and it was fun. She drank some more of her wine, feeling pleasantly tipsy. The dessert menu had arrived and been refused, and she thought that she had ordered coffee, although she wasn't quite sure.

'Yes, you're absolutely right. Very vain.' His wicked brown eyes swept over her and he grinned. 'I'm thirty-four but, deep down, I'm still a kid who kinda likes the idea of seeing himself hanging on a wall in my house. What do you think? Do you think I'd make a good sitter?'

'Sophie doesn't go for blonds, Adrian.' Rafe's voice was soft but sharp.

'Excuse me?' she said, turning to him. He was so close to her that she could feel his breath against her face. He wasn't looking at her, though. His eyes were narrowed on Adrian, with just the merest hint of a smile to tone down the warning in them.

'Besides, what's happened to the little Spanish beauty you were with a few weeks ago?'

'Galloped back to Spain,' Adrian said mournfully, 'leaving a broken heart behind.'

'Anyone's in particular?' The uncomfortable moment passed, and the conversation became good-humoured, with Rafe relaxing back once more and signalling for the bill.

It seemed almost disappointing that the evening was over. She would stick the outrageous dress back into her wardrobe and who knew when it would make a second appearance?

On a sudden tide of self-pity, she reached for the remnants of wine in her glass, as everyone was standing up to leave, and she felt Rafe's hand descend to circle her wrist.

'I think you've had enough,' he said under his breath.

'I don't care what you think,' Sophie muttered mutinously, looking at his lean brown fingers and feeling a spurt of confused rebellion well up inside her.

'Well, in the morning you'll care about what *you* think of yourself.' He curled his arm around her waist, supporting her as they all trooped towards the door, and once outside, the darkness provided welcome cover for her wobbly legs.

How much had she drunk? she wondered? It had seemed to be only a glass or two, but then the very efficient wine waiter had been topping them all up throughout the course of the evening. She became aware that she was leaning against Rafe and tried to pull herself away, but his arm was like an iron grip.

The couples had already departed in their pre-booked taxis and she was unsteadily aware of Adrian, leaning to kiss her on her cheek and whispering in her ear that he would be in touch.

Then the three of them were on the pavement, with George patiently waiting in the Jag, the embodiment of discretion.

'I need to get a cab,' Sophie said, looking around and feeling a bit queasy. There didn't seem to be an abundance of them around, which would entail a walk, the very thought of which made her feel even sicker.

'Yes, you do,' Angela said, spinning round so that she was looking directly at Sophie. 'You look terrible. God, Rafe, is she for real?'

'Shut up, Angela!' His voice was like the crack of a whip

and Sophie cringed with embarrassment at the picture she was presenting. A very tarnished Cinderella, who was so unused to drinking that she was practically falling down after a few glasses! Angela had sipped nothing but mineral water for the duration of the evening. Sophie vaguely remembered her giving a run-down of her diet, which she had to adhere to because modelling was such a competitive world and one spare ounce of weight could spell the difference between success and failure. She had thought at the time how silly it was to deny yourself the things you enjoyed. Unfortunately, she was now heartily wishing that she had had the sense to control her sudden urge to enjoy the marvellous white wine in such steady supply. Unlike her, Angela still looked pristine, not a strand of hair out of place.

'Well, get her a taxi, then!' Angela snapped angrily. 'When you told me that she'd be joining us, I had no idea that you would end up having to babysit her!' Tears gathered in her eyes.

'We'll drop you back to your flat.' Rafe's voice was hard and flat. 'Then I'll see Sophie back to her place.'

'That's ridiculous!' Angela cried. 'Why can't she see herself home? And what about us? I thought we would be spending the night together!'

'I'll call you in the morning.' Without further preamble, he manoeuvred Sophie into the back seat, waited for Angela to slide in, then slammed the door shut behind them so that he could sit in the front, alongside his driver.

The drive to Angela's flat was completed in silence. Sophie rested her head against the window and closed her eyes, not wanting to see the resentment on the other woman's face, which, quite frankly, she understood. For Angela, her evening of fun followed by a romp in the hay with her lover had now been reduced to a night of solitude while the man who should have been at her side was busy on the other side of town delivering an inebriated last-minute guest back to her own place. Thinking too much about it threatened to release the headache that she could already feel gathering pace.

She was aware of the car stopping and the slamming of two doors as Rafe saw Angela to her front door. One peek was enough to tell her that the fight that Angela had initiated outside the restaurant was still in progress, although Rafe seemed to be contributing very little. All the talking and gestures were being conducted by Angela. He, on the other hand, stood quite still, hands tucked into his trouser pockets, head inclined slightly to one side.

She closed her eyes again to block out the depressing scenario. She knew she ought to rouse herself and tell him that she was fine, that she could take it from here, but she couldn't be bothered. Her limbs felt like lead and the alcohol was catching up fast, making her sleepy.

The next thing she was aware of was being lifted out of the car. By Rafe. That woke her up faster than a bucket of cold water thrown over her head and she began to wriggle.

'Put me down! I'm fully capable of walking!'

Without preamble, he dropped her to her feet and then waited as she giddily tried to regain her balance.

How much had she had to drink? Four glasses. No more. And he had been counting, aware of every sip she took even though his back might have been to her. He should have stopped her from having that last one, should have known from the heightened tempo of her voice and brightness of her eyes that she just wasn't accustomed to drinking and would end up just as she had, incapable of seeing herself home.

He watched as she managed a couple of unsteady steps

in the vague direction of the door, and then picked her up and slung her over his shoulder, ignoring the hands trying to pummel his back.

'I...I...how dare you? Put me down *this instant*!'

'Where are your keys?'

'I can't get them if I'm like this, can I?'

'Sure you can. Just hand them to me, because I'm not putting you down. I don't want to be responsible for you falling down and breaking something.'

Sophie awkwardly managed to retrieve the keys from her clutch bag, which was dangling ridiculously from her hands. Lord only knew what people would say if they could see her now. Draped over some man's shoulder like a sack of potatoes.

'I'm beginning to feel sick,' she complained.

'Keep it in. Which floor are you on?'

'Second.' If she had hoped that he might be daunted by the prospect of doing his caveman impersonation up two flights of stairs, she was disappointed, because he kicked the door shut behind him and carried her up as though she didn't weigh anything.

The house was dark and quiet. It was a large Victorian place that had been sectioned off into several small flats, each big enough to just about provide adequate cover space for one, very undemanding person. Sophie had been lucky to get hold of it because it was reasonably priced in a reasonably salubrious area.

She kept quite still as he fiddled with the key to her door, finally opening it, and positively sighed with relief when she was gently deposited on the bed in her room. He had thoughtfully avoided switching on the overhead light, opting instead for the table lamp on her small chest of drawers.

'I'll make you some coffee.'

'There's no need, Rafe.' She struggled into a sitting position on the bed, very much aware of the awful sight she must be making, with her coat still on and the wretched turquoise dress not looking quite so impressive as it had earlier on. 'Thank you for delivering me back here and I'm sorry…for spoiling your evening.' She enunciated every word very carefully and then subsided back onto the pillows and covered her face with her arm.

Sleep was just beginning to seduce her when she felt herself being shaken and then helped up, back into that sitting position that made her head throb and eyeballs ache.

'Take these.'

'Why are you still here?'

'Just take the painkillers, Sophie. If you don't, your hangover tomorrow morning is going to hurt even more.' He thrust the tablets into one hand and a glass of water into the other and watched while she swallowed the tablets. 'Now let's get you out of your coat.' He didn't give her time to protest, just eased it off it, shuffling her a bit so that he could slide it out from under her and toss it on the chair by the door. 'Right. Now the shoes.' He was squatting by the bed, looking at her. He should be furious at having his plans for the night changed because of her antics, but instead he just felt amused at the sight of her sullen face and that hair curling wildly over her shoulders and down her back.

'I don't see the joke!' Sophie snapped, reading his expression. She hiccupped, which was annoying, and continued to glare at him.

'This isn't exactly how I imagined spending my evening,' Rafe drawled, straightening up and sitting on the bed next to her.

'I know and I'm sorry.' Embarrassment and guilt rushed over her, followed swiftly by anger because, really, there had been no need for him to deliver her like a package to her room. She hadn't asked him to and, the longer he stayed, the more humiliated she felt. She also remembered his little quip about lifting her up because he didn't want to be responsible for her falling over and hurting herself. As though she were a toddler in need of a steadying hand! 'Your girlfriend was very cross and I don't blame her,' Sophie said, going down the appeasing route, the quicker to get rid of him. 'Good Lord, I feel ill. Please, just go.'

'You need to get out of that dress. Where do you keep your...whatever it is you sleep in?' He stood up and headed for the chest of drawers, which appeared to have nothing he could identify as something a woman would sleep in. It took him a few minutes to realise that he wasn't dealing with a woman of the sort he was familiar with, but a woman whose dress code barely seemed to have struggled into the twenty-first century. Little wisps of black lace and sexy French knickers would not be on the sartorial menu, never mind that she had broken out of her routine tonight. He glanced across to where she had clearly fallen asleep and for a few seconds contemplated the turquoise-clad figure, arm still protectively covering her face, her chest rising and falling rhythmically. Her dress had risen provocatively higher, so that most of her thigh was exposed and just the merest sliver of underwear.

He felt something tighten in him and with a muttered, impatient oath he resumed his searching of the drawers until he extracted something big, old, stretchy and distinctly unappealing, which could only be classed as nightwear for the sleeping Cinderella.

She would probably go into one of her funks the next morning, but she would thank him deep down for not letting her sleep in that very tight dress. And, like it or not, she was his responsibility. After all, their mothers were close friends! She had been thrust upon him but, now that she was here, he had a duty to make sure that she was all right. He wondered what his mother would say if could see the situation now. What *both* their mothers would say!

She barely woke as he eased her out of the cling film. A few soft moans, but she was as pliable as a rag doll, allowing him to peel the dress down, down past her smooth, pale shoulders, sprinkled with freckles to match her face, down lower.

The tightness he had felt earlier on came back with a thunderous, physical rush as he eased the dress lower and realised, too late, that there was no gossamer-thin strapless bra supporting her breasts. Pert, as pale as the rest of her, crowned with pink nipples that were tipped up at him. He had seen sufficient breasts in his life to know what they looked like, but he could still feel his face suffusing with colour and was damned glad that the lighting in the room was dim, just in case she woke up.

Then he thought that if she *did* wake up, his bloody adolescent embarrassment would be wiped clean off his face by the crack of her hand against his cheek.

This was the kid next door? The woman with the dubious taste in clothing? The one who followed him around against his wishes and felt free to voice her opinions even when he clearly wasn't interested?

He disrobed her in record time, but very gently so that he didn't wake the sleeping tiger. His body was doing crazy things, which he tried to squash by telling himself that he was highly irritated at finding himself in the uninvited role of caretaker to a kid who couldn't hold her drink, and by ignoring those breasts as he eased the baggy nightdress over her head. Mission accomplished, he sprang back and walked towards the door before pausing to cast one last glance at the prone figure on the bed. Out for the count and snoring softly. Never mind the dress removal, he grinned to himself, any mention of snoring, softly or otherwise, would probably provoke the same outraged response.

On impulse, he scribbled a few words on some paper he found by her telephone and left the note propped up on the chest of drawers. She couldn't fail to see it first thing in the morning.

She did see it. Just about the same time as her memory of the night before began playing in her head, starting with her entrance into the restaurant and ending with her being bundled back to her flat by a very annoyed Rafe who had seen plans for his night with Angela scuppered by his misguided sense of responsibility.

She groaned and sat up and, in between the thought of getting out of bed to fetch his note and actually doing something about it, she realised that she was no longer in her dress. She was in her old, worn nightie and since the only person to accompany her to her flat was Rafe…

Heat started from the tips of her toes and worked its way remorselessly up her body. The body that had been sheathed in that tight dress, the *bra-less* body that had been sheathed in that tight dress…

She would have vaulted out of bed to get to the note, but her head didn't allow for too much unnecessary movement. She took it very easy, giving herself plenty of time to replay the disaster that had been last night.

She had been the belle of the ball, or at least she had felt like it—especially once that smooth white wine had started having an effect. She remembered feeling utterly relaxed and laughing a lot and being complimented by a very nice man with blond hair. Rafe had been sitting next to her. That had been the fly in the ointment, but she had ignored him, even though she had been fiercely conscious of him inches away from her. And then Angela, who had hit the roof when it had dawned on her that she would be returning to her apartment without her escort.

In the cold, sober light of day, events seemed rather different. She had felt like a different person, true enough, but what a complete fool she must have made of herself, behaving utterly out of character and then ending the evening by having to be chaperoned home like a teenager whose behaviour had become embarrassingly out of hand. Her mind braked to a crashing stop at events that unfolded after that, which she couldn't recall firsthand, but which her imagination was only too willing to fill in.

Her heart sank further at the contents of the note. No recriminations. Just a gentle command that she take it easy for the morning and meet him for lunch at an Italian café in Knightsbridge. Because he needed to have a little chat with her.

For the remainder of what was left of the morning, Sophie's mind went into runaway mode at the prospect of what that little chat might be about. Whatever it was, it wouldn't be good. Little chats never were. At worst, she would walk away even more humiliated than she currently felt. More than she had felt when she had been an infatuated teenager and he had told her, politely but firmly, to get lost.

But she couldn't run away. Sooner or later she would come crash, bang into him at one of his mother's summer barbecues or Christmas parties, which she always seemed to find herself coerced into attending. And then there was the small matter of the assignment, a favour from his mother. To run away would be to let her mother down, his mother down, the company down, and herself as well, although she thought that she would probably not lose too much sleep if she were the only person involved.

With a trapped feeling, she found herself heading off for

the restaurant at exactly eleven-thirty. On the bright side, her head had cleared up. On the other hand, her stomach had taken over where the head had left off, twisting into queasy knots as the bus deposited her too close to the restaurant for her liking.

She had returned to her comfort clothes, in a conscious effort to distance herself from the person of the night before. She was even carrying her smart briefcase, although she couldn't conceive of any situation arising whereby she might possibly want to take notes.

She spotted Rafe almost as soon as she walked in. There was a bar dominating one wall of the restaurant, which was not modelled on traditional lines, and there he was, sitting on one of the bar stools and nursing a glass of something.

And he looked amazing. Cool, sexy, expensive. Sophie had thought about what she would say, how she would apologise for her behaviour, but looking at him now, she knew that any apology would be a big mistake. He didn't want or need some woman snivelling on his shoulder like a child. If he saw her as a liability and wanted to end their informal arrangement, then any show of vulnerable behaviour would just reinforce his decision, and, really, it would be awful to have him think of her as that drippy little woman who needed rescuing.

Then she thought of him getting her out of that dress, his hands brushing against her naked body while she blissfully slept on, and it took a huge effort not to falter in her brisk stride towards the bar.

'Hi,' she said brightly, eyes sliding away from him towards the man serving behind the bar.

'Feeling okay today?' Rafe drawled, sipping his drink slowly and looking at her over the rim of his glass with those green, green eyes.

'Oh, you know, the head was pounding this morning but

nothing that a couple of painkillers couldn't take care of!'
She hoped that her voice struck exactly the right chord of
experience at life's little foibles and amusement by them.
'Shall I sit at the bar or is there a table reserved for us?
Popular place, isn't it? But I guess that's to be expected
considering it's in Knightsbridge.'

'Table, I think.' He seemed to make invisible yet obvious
compelling eye contact with someone, because no sooner
was he off his bar stool, than a young waiter was scurrying
over to them with menus under his arm.

He allowed her to precede him and sighed under his
breath. He had contemplated ignoring the whole business
of the night before, but had decided against it. He had never
volunteered for role of caretaker before, but what choice
did he have? She wasn't some random stranger whose irritating presence he could dispense with, or more likely
delegate to his secretary to dispense with while he continued his fast-rolling life of work. Under normal circumstances he wouldn't have given a second thought to what
the outcome for her might have been had he dispensed with
her. He would have eliminated her as unsound for her job.

He had a flashback to the sight of her, as limp as a rag
doll as he eased her dress off her, and his momentary reaction to seeing those breasts, innocently exposed.

He frowned, irritated at being reminded of that fleeting
moment when, for once, all his control had flown out of
the window and in its place had been something dark and
confusing and unsettling.

'Right,' he said abruptly, shifting his chair sideways so
that he could cross his legs, 'we need to talk.'

CHAPTER FOUR

SOPHIE felt her stomach lurch. It reminded her of that sea-sick feeling she had experienced as a young teenager when she had gone on a cross-channel school trip to France, but without the happy knowledge that sooner or later the ship would dock and the sickness would disappear. She had the nasty suspicion that whatever Rafe said now would haunt her for ever.

She bit back the urge to rush into instant, hand-wringing apology and offered him a polite, interested smile.

'I wouldn't normally be inclined to dredge up embarrassing incidents...' Rafe leaned forward, elbows on the table, his fabulous face rueful but firm. 'However, we need to talk about what happened last night.'

Sophie took a deep breath and said quietly, 'I'm very sorry if I embarrassed you in front of your friends.'

She had half expected him to use that as his opening cue to lay into her, but instead he sat back and looked at her with amusement, which seemed more irritating than the response she had predicted. Instinct told her to hold onto her annoyance and run with it, but common sense thankfully prevailed, and she frowned.

'I don't see what's so funny...'

'Why do you imagine that your behaviour, or anyone else's for that matter, might embarrass me? Besides, believe me when I tell you that I've seen far worse. No...you surprised me, but I wasn't embarrassed.'

'I *surprised* you? How did I surprise you?' Her ruffled

feathers were temporarily calmed by his prosaic reaction.

And if he wasn't going to deliver a speech on her ridiculous behaviour, then what exactly was this chat, so-called, going to be about?

Rafe took his time answering that question. For once, he was in no huge rush, having had his early afternoon appointment cancelled because the director of the company was laid up with some ridiculous bug that was going round. He gave the waitress time to take their orders, time to pour him a glass of wine. Sophie, he noticed, was sticking to water.

'Would you like a long answer or the abridged version?' He sipped some of his wine and looked at her over the rim of his glass. Her look was telling him that she would rather he avoided the subject altogether, but in the absence of that possibility he knew that she would go for the long answer. Experience with women had long left him to conclude that they enjoyed hearing about themselves whenever possible.

He was slightly taken aback when she shrugged and concluded in a weary voice that, since he was going to tell her anyway, he might as well decide how elaborate he wanted his answer to be.

'You surprised me when you appeared wearing next to nothing…'

Sophie reddened. 'I was not wearing *next to nothing*! In fact, the saleswoman assured me that it was a very popular style! I'm not exactly ancient, you know. I don't have to confine myself to long-sleeved dresses that reach down to my ankles.'

'No, but you normally do,' Rafe pointed out, enjoying her little flurry of self-defence. In fact, enjoying the uncustomary sensation of having a meal in the middle of the day without having to continually watch the hands of the clock ticking their way through his snatched leisure time. 'Put it this way: every time I've seen you in the past at one of my mother's little do's—'

'Your mother's do's are never little.'

'I stand corrected. But, getting back to the point, I've never seen you in anything smaller than a long skirt or a pair of baggy trousers, even in the height of summer.'

Sophie experienced a moment of true horror as she thought of him glancing at her from the cosy coterie of his sophisticated, well-dressed clique and catching sight of her in one of her speciality flowing outfits, which she had always thought eminently suitable when confronted with an outdoor party in the height of an English summer.

'I've never seen the point of trying to manoeuvre a lawn in high-heeled stilettos and tight dresses,' she retorted.

'Sensible,' he concurred, and she glared at him, not caring for that word *sensible*, which reeked of *boring*. 'So it was quite surprising when you turned up in that little blue outfit. I suppose I should be flattered that you wore it for my benefit...' Rafe had no idea what mischievous thought had made him say that, but he felt a shocking little buzz when she blushed. It made her look defiant and sheepish at the same time.

She had had a crush on him when she was a kid, following him around with her sheep's eyes whenever he had come back on his holidays. He lazily played with the notion that perhaps that crush had been lying there, dormant, waiting for a suitable opportunity to rear its head once again...and what better opportunity than enforced confinement with him over a two-week period?

'It wasn't for your benefit, Rafe,' Sophie said calmly. 'I know you probably think that every woman can't help but fluff her feathers up when you're around, but I bought that dress because I didn't want to embarrass you in front of your friends.' There was sufficient truth in that for her voice to remain steady. 'I know I don't dress in the height of fashion. Blame my parents. They always told me that it was what's inside that counted, that it was sad to mindlessly follow fashion just because everyone else was doing it. But you had invited me to a social gathering and I'm not stupid. I know lots of people don't share my opinions. I mean, you for one.'

The accusation, coming from nowhere, brought all amusing thoughts to an abrupt halt. He narrowed his eyes and stared at her for a few unsettling seconds.

'Care to explain where you're going with that?'

'My job here…' *if I still have a job here,* she thought '…is to observe you. Not just the working man, but to form an impression of the whole man, the complete picture, so to speak.'

'And your complete picture is…?' His voice was cool enough to halt a charging rhino in its tracks.

Which suggested that it was all right for him to vocalise sweeping statements about her, but not too acceptable when the shoe was on the other foot. Oh, well. If his little chat revolved around packing her back off to oblivion, then she might as well go out with a bang.

'That you are entirely focused and driven when it comes to work. Too driven, I would say, but of course that's just my personal opinion.' She could feel her momentum gathering pace as the food was placed in front of them. Ravioli for her and fish for him, both mouth-wateringly tempting. She gratefully stabbed some of the pasta with her fork, avoiding eye contact.

'Go on. I'm all ears.'

Funny, she thought, how the literal meaning of his words could offer encouragement while his tone of voice managed to take it away.

'I gather you don't give yourself time to form any lasting relationships with women, hence your unmarried status.' Her voice faltered in the face of his continuing silence. She took another deep, bracing breath.

'Or perhaps I'm of that rare breed of man who doesn't see the value of rushing into something as important as marriage because society dictates that it's time.'

'That's not the impression I get.'

'You are overstepping your brief.'

Sophie risked a glance. His expression was unreadable but his mouth was unsmiling. 'I don't have a brief, Rafe.'

'Fine. Well, how's this for a compromise? You voice your opinions, but I will not tolerate idle speculation being printed about me. In other words, you print facts, not bits of fiction that you've knitted together in an attempt to read my personality. Got it?'

'Where does the fact end and the fiction begin?'

'Fact: I work hard. Fiction: I am somehow missing out on fun. Fact: I am single. Fiction: It is because I work too hard to be interested in getting married and settling down to a house in the suburbs with the regulatory two point two children, dog and, in time, a mistress in the city. Fact: I rarely go on holiday. Fiction: It is because I have lost the art of enjoying leisure time. Are you getting the drift?'

'Why would you have a mistress if you were married?' Sophie asked, shocked by the depth of cynicism contained in that one passing phrase.

'Oh, for God's sake, Sophie.' Rafe closed his knife and fork, sat back and tossed his napkin to the side of his plate. 'Your father was a vicar, but surely you must have grown up with some idea of how the world works!'

'Maybe that's how it works in the circles you mix in…'

'It's the nature of man,' Rafe gritted out, very slowly.

'Human beings are not monogamous creatures. If you want my honest opinion, people rush into marriages for all the wrong reasons, hence the unhealthy divorce rate!'

'All the wrong reasons, such as love? Affection? Devotion?'

'Aren't you missing out one vital reason?' His mouth curved into a slow, knowing smile that sent little shivers racing up and down her spine. 'Plain old lust. You can't beat it. Sadly, it tends to get confused with other, nobler sentiments and that's the problem. Relationships start out fine and dandy and if you're not careful you start thinking that, because you can't wait to hop in the sack with someone, then it must be something lasting and wonderful. Then the lust factor starts getting tarnished round the edges and, before you know it, the whole thing's gone belly up and you're left with two warring adults, unhappy children and, usually in the man's case, alimony repayment till the day he dies.'

'Can I quote that?' Sophie asked lightly and he shot her an irritated frown.

'Not word for word, but you can use the general sentiment.'

'As an excuse for your single state…'

'No one needs an *excuse* to remain single. Just a healthy dose of common sense.'

'Maybe you just haven't met the right woman,' Sophie mused, risking a glance. She just couldn't picture Rafael Loro with the right woman because that would mean losing that formidable self-control of his, being vulnerable to someone else. *Rafe* and *vulnerable* weren't two words that went together. It was a bit like linking *shark* with *tender-hearted*. She couldn't help a ghost of a smile from forming and Rafe, who never missed a thing, was quick to catch on.

'Share the joke.' Of course she was as innocent as the day was long. It showed in those half-baked romantic notions of hers, but he still found it annoying to have her level that vaguely pitying look at him, as though she had managed to find the secret key to the meaning of life. He scowled and beckoned across a waiter so that he could order a cafetière of coffee.

'There's no joke,' Sophie said, fixing her features. 'So you haven't got married, not because you believe in it and you're waiting for the right woman. You haven't got married because on paper it's an institution that just has too many things going against it.'

Rafe inclined his head to one side. 'You're sensible with your clothes,' he drawled, 'and I'm sensible when it comes to women.'

Sophie wondered whether he had meant to sound insulting or whether it had been an unconscious arrangement of words. It didn't matter. The effect was the same. She still felt nettled.

'Is that why you date women like Angela?' she ventured recklessly.

Rafe swung round to look at her. 'In case you hadn't noticed, she's a very sexy woman.' Admittedly not so sexy that he had raced over to see her last night, even though he had conceivably had time. It just proved his point that lust was a passing phase. Six months ago he had not been able to get enough of her. He thought with some degree of satisfaction that he was utterly in control of his emotions and thereby in control of his life, then it occurred to him that the woman sitting opposite him would probably launch into another debate on the subject. It was slightly surprising that he had allowed her to get as far as she had voicing her opinions. He decided that

that was simply an example of his fairness. After all, she was just doing her job.

He also realised that he still hadn't got round to the little chat he was determined to have and was now in danger of running late for his three o'clock meeting.

'She doesn't seem very challenging,' Sophie said eventually, and he gave her a slow grin.

'No, not mentally challenging, perhaps...'

Which wasn't to say that she wasn't deeply challenging on other fronts, his look seemed to imply.

'Has Claudia met her as yet?'

Rafe looked suitably horrified, then he grinned conspiratorially at Sophie. 'Come on, Sophie. You know my mother. What do you think?'

Sophie thought that suddenly there was a thread of intimacy running between them that was a little nerve-racking. 'She might like her,' she said neutrally, and his grin broadened. When he smiled like that, without any cynicism or mockery, he was mind-blowingly attractive.

'Or she might not. I've gone for the latter option.' The grin became a low laugh. 'The last time I took a woman back home, a woman very much like Angela, now I come to think of it, I had to suffer the discomfort of my mother trying her hardest to break all conversations down to their simplest terms and then a post-mortem that included a lot of disappointed sighs and heartfelt advice about thinking hard before getting too involved with her. Poor Fiona Blythe-White. She only lasted another fortnight.'

Sophie couldn't help herself. She burst out laughing, imagining the scenario. Claudia was as sharp as a knife. She would have struggled with a bimbo.

She had a laugh as full-bodied as her opinions, Rafe thought, disconcerted for a few seconds. She wasn't by nature an extrovert or naturally someone who revelled in being the centre of attention, but there was a sincerity in everything she said and did that was refreshing.

He looked at his watch and, catching the direction of his gaze, Sophie said, with amusement still in her voice, 'I'm sorry. You must be getting back to the office. I know you normally have meetings lined up every afternoon.'

'I had a cancellation. Raymond Slater's off with some bug or other.'

'How inconsiderate of him,' Sophie teased and he responded with a wry smile.

'Exactly what I was thinking.'

'Can you tell me what the outcome was of your meeting with Bob Beardsman? I know I won't be around to see the outcome of that meeting, but I would be interested in knowing. Has he decided to sell to you?'

'We're both still sitting on it.'

'Well, you'll have to fill me in some time...not that our paths will cross in the near future...' Her voice dwindled off and she felt an inexplicable chill race through her, which was silly, of course. 'You meant to have a chat with me. Do you have time? Would you rather leave it until Monday?'

'I'm away on Monday.' Where the hell had the time gone?

'And is it that important?'

Rafe thought of her and her innocence, her romantic notions. *Damned important.*

'Yes,' he said bluntly. Their coffees were finished and the bill had been brought to the table, but instead of paying he ordered two more coffees and a slab of chocolate cake with cream. He had expected her to shake her head and refuse but, after a moment of surprise, she seemed happy enough to plough her way through some dessert. In fact, her eyes positively lit up when it was placed in front of her, and, despite the *little chat* that he knew he now had to accomplish in record time, he couldn't resist asking her how it was that she had managed to avoid the irritating female complaint of being on a perpetual diet.

'Not vain enough, I guess,' Sophie said, shrugging and enjoying every mouthful of sinful, calorie-laden heaven. 'That's another advantage of wearing comfortable, baggy clothes, you see. They can hide a multitude of sins.'

Not that there were any on view last night, Rafe thought, remembering how that dress had clung to every inch of her slender body. He realised that she was looking at him curiously and also realised that he had lapsed into silence, contemplating her, her dress and his removal of it.

He shook himself out of his unexpected reverie.

'I don't quite know how to broach this subject,' he began slowly and Sophie paused, forkful of cake *en route* to her mouth, which was parted slightly in anticipation of savouring it. Her heart sank. Lunch had been so much better than she had expected. She might have known that the temporary camaraderie had been just a lull before the storm because Rafael Loro was not a man who baulked at broaching any subject. Suddenly the cake no longer tasted as exquisite as it had done seconds before, although she made herself finish the lot, pushing the plate away from her and wiping her mouth with her napkin.

'I wouldn't normally be giving this speech if...' he frowned and looked at her thoughtfully '...if we didn't go back a long way.'

Well, there was no response to that, was there? Sophie looked at him, bewildered and already miserably planning what she would say to her boss about her failed enterprise.

And what it would feel like to walk into another office, one that wasn't filled with his dynamic presence... She was gripped suddenly by a cold feeling of dread.

'Look, I'll just spit it out. I watched you last night…and you haven't got a clue, have you?'

'A clue about what?' Her eyes widened as she tried to puzzle out what he was trying to tell her.

'A clue about what London is really like. It's a jungle and you're no jungle animal. I saw that firsthand last night. You were dressed in clothes that would attract a blind man, you had too much to drink and you were provocative.'

Sophie's mouth dropped open and a slow flush crawled into her cheeks as she began to decipher where he was going.

'I—I wasn't…provocative…' she stammered.

'Adrian Walsh was all over you, Sophie. I don't normally put myself in a position of feeling responsible for other people's behaviour, but, like I said, I've known you since you were a kid—'

'And I'm not one now!' The delicate flush had become two angry, concentrated red patches on her cheeks. 'I can look after myself, Rafe! There's no need for you to feel responsible for me!'

'Are you trying to convince me that you're so capable of looking after yourself that I had to drop you home and get you to bed? Do you have any idea what kind of position you put yourself into?'

'I was perfectly capable of getting home by myself!'

'Rubbish. You could hardly walk a straight line.'

Had everyone else seen her in the same way? As a country bumpkin who had somehow bungled her way into their élite, private party and proceeded to make a fool of herself? She went hot all over just thinking about it.

'I got home to a message on my answer machine. Adrian wanting your telephone number. What exactly did you say to him?'

'I didn't say anything to him! I chatted! It's hardly my

fault if he got the wrong idea! And you can't blame my clothes,' she added, with a flash of brilliance. 'Angela wasn't exactly bundled up! Do you feel responsible for her as well? In fact, do you feel responsible for every woman you see wearing a short skirt and having a bit to drink?'

'Don't be bloody ridiculous.'

'I'm not being ridiculous, Rafe! I'm just trying to make you see that there's no need for you to feel responsible for me.' She could have added that it was a downright insult. 'You keep calling me *sensible*. Now you're treating me like a kid. Make your mind up! Either I'm a sensible adult or I'm an irresponsible kid!'

Rafe shook his head impatiently and then fixed his brooding eyes on her. 'What would have happened if Adrian had escorted you back to your flat instead of me?'

She knew exactly where he was going with that silky soft question and it made her skin burn. She frantically tried to think of something biting to say, and he filled the intervening silence.

'Adrian is a predator and predators don't normally have much in the way of the gentlemanly instinct.'

'Birds of a feather...' she mumbled, and Rafe leaned forward, his mouth thinning.

'Meaning?'

'Nothing.' She dropped her eyes, avoiding his, but she could still feel his glass-green stare burning into her. It took huge effort, but she managed to control all the emotions flooding her and think about what she was being paid by her company to do—her extremely optimistic, trusting and *new* company. 'Thank you for your consideration,' she managed to choke out, 'and for your advice. I'll make sure I remember it in future.' *Every time I want to feel really small and insecure,* she added silently to herself.

'No way.'

'No way what?' Sophie looked at him and received the full blast of his intensity.

'No way are you going to make a remark like that about me without qualifying it, and don't even pretend that you don't know what I'm talking about. You spoke of me in the same breath as Adrian. Are you implying that I am a predator as well?'

'If the cap fits…' Sophie met that stare head-on.

'Then I would be sure to wear it.' He leaned towards her and the slight shift in his body posture seemed to bring him dangerously close. 'But it doesn't and I want you to tell me why you think it does.'

Sophie shrugged. 'I guess you both see women as fair game and not as potential partners. At least, that's what it sounds like from what you have said about Adrian. I don't remember having an opinion one way or another.'

'Adrian would not have undressed you and then left your apartment,' Rafe said bluntly. 'Trust me.'

'Why do you socialise with him if your opinion of him is so low?'

'I did some business with him a while back. He's a web designer, and, believe it or not, he has a good sense of humour. Invaluable asset when your working days are generally devoid of humour. That, however, does not mean that I am like him in any way.' For some reason it was irritating to find himself lumped in the same category as someone who was an amusing but inveterate player. And yet again he had digressed from the whole point of the exercise, which was to deliver, very gently of course, one or two home truths on looking after herself in the big, bad world.

He couldn't imagine Grace being anything but worried sick about her daughter living in London.

She had always been a very protective mother, for goodness' sake! What had she been thinking, sending her Sophie to the city on her own? Didn't she know that that youthful innocence could appeal to any number of womanisers or perverts?

'Okay,' Sophie agreed readily. 'Shall we go now? I know you must have your diary blocked out for the rest of the afternoon. I thought, actually, that I might use what's left of the day to edit what I've written so far. Would I be able to use that vacant office again?'

Rafe, still fulminating over Grace's recklessness in letting her daughter loose in London, barely heard Sophie until she repeated herself, then he stared at her narrowly.

'Of course, I will not be passing your phone number on to Adrian,' he remarked, frowning heavily at her.

Sophie opened her mouth to tell him that it was up to her whether she got in touch with Adrian or not, her choice to make, and then thought better of it. Why antagonise him further? Yes, it was offensive to think that he was setting himself up as some sort of counsellor for her, because she was obviously too ignorant and naïve to take care of herself, but on the other hand she could do without the attentions of a womaniser. She uneasily wondered how well she would be able to take care of herself, though she would never have admitted that in a thousand years. Rafe lecturing from the moral high ground was certainly in need of no ammunition.

'That's fine.'

For an inoffensive answer, she was surprised at his reaction. Instead of relaxing, his expression darkened and he grated, 'Would that be because you already have a man in tow? I have enough experience of women to know that they sometimes cover up secrets they don't want other people to know about, and an undesirable man lurking in the background usually fits that description.'

Sophie, enraged by the accusation, wondered whether he had finally taken leave of his senses, and her outraged expression said as much. He relaxed.

'Just making sure,' he purred, signalling for the bill while she watched him in disbelief. 'Now, you were saying about that office and whether you could use it. Sure. Or you could use mine, of course. I won't be in for the rest of the afternoon and, as I said, on Monday I'm away for the day. You're more than welcome to accompany me, but you'll find seven hours cooped up with a team of lawyers staggeringly boring.'

Sophie wondered whether staggeringly boring came close to staggeringly arrogant.

The man never stopped surprising her. Just when she found herself relaxing, he changed course and afforded her a brutal reminder of exactly how dislikeable he could be. She should have known from the start that their histories were too entwined for him ever to see her as anything but a kid. She needed to be viewed as an equal, and sometimes it really felt as though he was doing that, but then they came bouncing back to square one and it was infuriating.

She watched in stony silence as he settled the bill, refusing her offer to pay her way without even bothering to look up.

'Just out of interest,' she asked coldly as they walked out towards the Jaguar, which was parked obligingly close to the restaurant, 'what happens when my assignment here is finished and you're no longer around to keep a beady eye on me and dish out health and safety warnings? Do you think that I might succumb to any passing pervert because I'm too simple to look out for myself?'

'Not if you pay attention to my advice,' Rafe said, opening the car door for her and waiting until they were both inside before continuing. 'You have to learn to be careful,' he informed her in a tone of voice that made her hackles rise still further. 'A scantily clad, fairly inebriated, attractive young woman is a magnet for any man who wants to take advantage.'

'I can't believe you're telling me this.'

'Believe me, it is not in my nature to try and tell people how to behave—'

'But you will do anyway!'

'What choice do I have?' He spread his hands magnanimously and Sophie wanted to list all the choices he had, including keeping out of her private life, but somehow she knew that protests from her would not deter him from his crusade. 'My mother would want it. Who knows…' He shrugged one elegant shoulder and gave her a rueful smile. 'Maybe that is why she recommended you to me?'

'That is the—most—preposterous thing I have ever heard.'

'You say that, but it makes sense…' She looked as though she might explode with rage any minute. Her cheeks were flushed and she was quivering. Rafe thought of those women he dated, the beautiful Angelas who glided elegantly through life, rarely seeming to react to the whole business of Life. Sophie was a world apart. She seemed to react to every nuance. He had never seen anything like it.

In a minute, she would hit him. He could see it from the way she was curling her fists on her lap, as if willing herself to step back and not give in totally to her emotions.

And what would he do if she *did* hit him? he wondered.

It wouldn't be the first time, he mused to himself. And every other time he had simply walked away. Hysterical women left him cold. This time, though…

He shot her a brooding stare from under his lashes. 'New to London. Inexperienced. My mother would have known that having me keep an eye on you for a couple of weeks would do you good.'

He smiled at her with such patronising kindness that Sophie wanted to scream. Instead, she made an inarticulate, strangled sound.

'I am not *entirely* inexperienced, Rafe,' she said through gritted teeth. 'While you were climbing the ladder and adding to your millions, I wasn't sitting at home knitting scarves and going to bed at nine!'

Rafe's expression changed to one of lively interest and she could have kicked herself for being provoked into reacting. He just seemed to have a knack of having that effect on her.

'No?'

'No.' Sophie firmly doused his curiosity with a quelling look.

'What were you doing?' He shook his head and looked at her gravely. 'You disillusion me, Sophie Frey. I never thought you were a wild child.'

'I am *not* a wild child! Look, I don't even know why we're talking about this!' With a great wave of relief, she saw that George was pulling up to the offices, where she would be dropped off before Rafe continued across London, and Rafe, following the direction of her glance, was almost disappointed to note that they had arrived.

How many times had he cursed the London traffic and sworn that he would escape to a more civilised place as soon as he could? Now, just when a spot of traffic would have allowed him to pursue this very illuminating conversation, they had managed to clear the city in record time.

He belatedly reminded himself that it was just as well considering he was running late.

Her hand was already on the door handle before the car had time to pull to a complete stop. 'We're here!'

'So I see,' Rafe drawled dryly. 'Try not to collapse with the sheer excitement of getting away from our conversation.' He didn't think he could ever remember a time when a woman had been so keen to escape his company. And the conversation had been about *her*!

Sophie, with the door already open and one foot poised outside, could feel generous on the point of departure. She half turned to him and smiled. Warmly, she hoped.

'Don't be silly! I wasn't trying to get away from you. I'm very grateful for your concern, in fact. I'll be sure to report home what a good father-figure you're turning out to be. And I'll see you on Tuesday!'

Rafe was still frowning at the insult, fully deserved though it was, when the car door slammed, leaving him nursing the unpleasant feeling that he had just been outwitted by the last person in the world he would have expected it to come from.

CHAPTER FIVE

THE weekend was long enough for Sophie to get things into perspective. Rafe and his wretched speech had come like a bolt from the blue because he was just the last person she would have associated with the finer feelings of thoughtfulness and consideration. The last person, in fact, she would have *wanted* to display those qualities because, coming from him, they were an implied insult.

But they could only undermine her if she allowed it.

She should, she knew, accept his well-intentioned, caring advice in the spirit in which it was intended and ignore the persistent voice in her head that was sniggering madly and telling her that the leggy, beautiful, sharp-as-nails Angela would never have been subject to a fatherly protective instinct. True, she hadn't foreseen it, but, thinking about it, it had been inevitable. He hadn't wanted her around, was stuck in a mindset that still saw her as the gauche teenager gazing longingly at him from a distance. So, after the initial antipathy, he would naturally position himself as the older, wiser figure, the mature counsellor whose duty was to take her under his wing.

The skin-tight blue dress, the alcohol, and the unexpected interest from Adrian hadn't helped matters, at least not as far as her staking her independence was concerned.

She would have to prove to him, in the remaining time she had left with him, that she was no longer that teenager. That she had never *been* that teenager. She had looked the part and she had had a silly crush on him once upon a time, but she had never been pathetic or helpless and she wasn't pathetic or helpless now.

She was waiting for his arrival on Tuesday, fortified by some good old-fashioned common sense, a mature look at the bigger picture and three days of not having him around, when Patricia, his secretary, came rushing into the temporary office where Sophie was doodling on a pad and thinking about how she could display herself in her best possible colours.

So far, she had not seen Patricia look anything but calm, measured and unflappable, even when Rafe had been storming around, restlessly barking orders and moving at the speed of light.

The sight of her now, in a distinct flap, was cause for worry.

In fact Sophie half rose from her chair, to be waved down by an agitated Patricia.

'It's Mr Loro!'

Sophie felt her face whiten as all the mature thoughts she had been diligently processing flew through the window. She leaned forward urgently. 'What's happened, Patricia? Has there been an accident? Is he...is he all right?' She had a sudden vision of Rafe caught up in a rubble of broken metal, his vital body shattered and lifeless. Nerve endings she'd never known she had reared into sensitive life, catapulting her body into painful overdrive.

'Yes. Oh, dear. I've worried you unduly.' Patricia took a few calming breaths and shut the door behind her, moving to sit in the chair opposite the desk. 'It's...well, Mr Loro has just called to inform me that he won't be coming in today and probably not for the rest of the week...'

Sophie felt faint with relief. The feeling was swiftly followed by irritation with Patricia that she had obviously made a mountain out of a molehill and with herself for her extreme reaction.

'Was there a problem with yesterday's meeting?' she asked, relaxing now. 'Must have been tricky if he's had to stay there for a couple of days.' Such was the aura of invincibility that he created around himself that it was almost impossible for her to imagine any situation he might find tricky.

'No, no problem. It's just that…he phoned in to say that he isn't well. You can imagine my shock! Mr Loro has never had a day off work, not in all the years I've worked with him. He's always had the stamina of a…a…'

'Bull?' Sophie volunteered helpfully. 'What's the matter with him?'

'Apparently there's some virus going around and he appears to have got it.' She allowed herself a small smile. 'It's almost nice to know that he's human after all. I hope you won't put that in your article!'

'Oh, I'm sure he would strike a line through it if I did.' Sophie smiled back at the older woman. 'He might be insulted to be called *human after all.*'

'The reason I flew in here,' Patricia carried on after a pause, 'is that Mr Loro specifically requested that you go over to see him.'

'He requested *what*?'

'Perhaps request isn't quite the word…'

'You mean I've been ordered to go to his house. Why?' As if she didn't know. What did he think she might get up to if he wasn't around for a couple of days? Mass subversion of his staff? Maybe he thought that she would encourage them to down tools and use the office building for an all-night rave?

'I don't know. This is an unprecedented situation. He did mention that there are a few documents he needs to have but, really, I could have taken them over, or I could have arranged for a courier to take them.' She looked as though she had been presented with a mathematical problem way outside her domain, one which she had not a hope in hell of solving.

'When did he want me over?' Sophie asked, resigned.

'Soon, sooner or soonest?'

'Soonest, I gather.' She deposited a stack of documents on the desk and stood up. 'Good luck.' This time the glance was sympathetic. 'He doesn't sound in the best of tempers.'

Does he ever? Sophie wondered.

London, as ever, lay in a pall of rain. The steady grey drizzle that had greeted her first thing when she had left her flat earlier on had decided to take a short coffee break, but it was leaving no one with any illusions that it had gone for the day. The skies were still leaden and there was the smell of damp in the air.

Fortunately, no public transport to worry about this time. Patricia had primed George and he was waiting in Reception for her, so she only had a quick sprint to the Jaguar, then blissful warmth once inside. She made some desultory conversation for a few minutes, then lapsed into silence, happy to stare out through the window and stoke her irritation at the thought of Rafe summoning her halfway across London. Wasn't this taking his babysitting duties too far? What next? Handwritten reports on her movements so that he could double-check them and make sure she was behaving herself? She was the one who was shadowing him, for goodness' sake!

The traffic was thick. The rain had turned the streets into a gluey mass of cars and taxis, which moved along in slow, unsatisfactory spurts, and it was a full hour before they finally arrived at their destination.

Sophie had no idea what she expected. It certainly wasn't

an unshaven Rafe, who answered the doorbell in his dressing gown and, while she was still standing on the doorstep, unsettled at the vision, turned his back and began walking towards a room off the hall.

Sophie followed at a rapid pace into a room that looked as though it had been designed for elegant relaxing rather than work. The long windows were dressed in deep red curtains, with Victorian shutters drawn back to allow as much watery light in as possible. The large sofa, which would have been too big for most rooms but fitted nicely into this one, had been turned into a makeshift bed, with the cushions piled up at one end, and the exquisite table that should have sat in the middle of the room had been dragged over and now housed several stacks of paper, a laptop computer, Rafe's cellular phone and various assorted items of stationery.

Sophie paused in the doorway, taking it all in, until Rafe said, irritably, 'Don't just stand there gawking.' He had dropped into one of the big chairs by the fireplace and was scowling at her.

Summoned out of her reverie, Sophie looked over in his direction, at the brown legs exposed by the bathrobe and the sliver of chest.

'Shouldn't you be properly…dressed if you're not well?' Originally she had planned on laying into him as soon as she arrived, demanding why he had seen fit to order her over to his house, accusing him of being offensive in his efforts to *keep an eye on her*, as if she were seven instead of twenty-seven.

Her plans had been scuppered by his semi-nudity. She found it hard to look at him at all, for fear of a detached glance turning into an avid, devouring stare. So she addressed the mantelpiece while remaining by the door.

'In a suit, you mean?' Rafe asked sarcastically. 'Which,

of course, is the attire of choice when at home ill?' His voice sounded throaty and, with some self-reproach, Sophie ventured into the room. Normally her compassionate nature would have kicked in by now, but, even ill, Rafe still managed to intimidate.

'I meant perhaps you should dress in something warmer.'

'I'm boiling hot, as it happens.'

'You probably have a fever.' She scuttled over to one of the chairs and sat down, resting the papers on her lap and her handbag at the side on the ground.

'Probably.'

'Have you taken anything for it?'

'I don't tend to keep flu medicine in the house. Believe it or not, this is the first time I can remember being ill since I was a child.' He frowned. 'Could you sit a bit closer? My throat hurts and shouting to you isn't going to do it any good. Actually, you might just as well go and buy me some tablets or whatever one takes in a situation like this.'

'The situation is called *having a cold*, Rafe. It's an annual event for most of us.' She looked down quickly because there was a bubble of laughter waiting to erupt inside her and she dreaded to think what his reaction would be to that. Poor Rafe, she sternly told herself. Of course he was finding it difficult to cope with a spot of ill health. Germs normally avoided him like the plague! That thought made her want to laugh even more. She stood up and fussed with the handbag at her feet, making sure that her face was perfectly composed when she finally turned to face him.

'I'll just pop out and get you something, then,' she said. 'Are you better with liquid or tablets?'

'Whatever's stronger,' Rafe muttered. 'I have to be back on my feet by tomorrow afternoon. I have a very important meeting.'

'Don't tell me that. Tell your virus,' Sophie informed

him, heading for the door. 'Although,' she threw over her shoulder, 'they have a nasty habit of not listening.'

'There's a corner shop just down the road,' was his response, and she waited until she was safely out of the house before she gave in to the fit of laughter that had been threatening for the past ten minutes.

She returned to find Rafe exactly where she had left him. His legs stretched out in front of him, and he was dozing lightly, although his eyes opened as soon as she walked through the door.

'You should get upstairs and try and sleep,' Sophie said, extracting a box from her bag and then proceeding to read the instructions on the back. 'You were nodding off just then. That's your body telling you that you need rest.'

'Don't be ridiculous. I was in the middle of finalising a report when you came in. My body will get rest when I tell it to and not a minute before. Never a good idea to sleep on the job, you know. Is that the medicine? What have you got there? Bring it over.'

'If you're not careful,' Sophie said, walking towards him, 'you are going to grow into a very crotchety old man, Rafael Loro. Snapping fingers and giving orders and grumbling.'

'Don't push your luck, Sophie. Our mothers might be good friends, but there is only so much psychobabble I can take. And another piece of advice for you: there's a fine line between preaching and nagging.'

But his voice was absent-minded as he took the bottle from her. Their fingers brushed and, with a slight frown, Sophie rested the back of her hand against his forehead.

'Lord, Rafe, you *have* got a fever! Look, hand me the bottle. It's a capful of this stuff.'

'I would have preferred the tablets, actually.' He held

onto the bottle and she looked at him incredulously. 'I'm not very good with this syrupy stuff, never have been.'

'Too bad. I'm not going back to the shop. It's beginning to rain again and it's cold out there.' She regained possession of the bottle, poured him a generous capful, and then folded her arms and watched as he drank the lot down with a telling grimace.

'There. Happy?'

'You're not taking this stuff for my benefit, Rafe. You're taking it for *yours*!' She moved quickly away, talking with her back to him. 'And you need to go up to your bed. Sitting down here, half dressed and pretending that you're going to get some work done, is just going to prolong this cold you've got.' She turned round and looked at him firmly, arms folded. He might not like her chivvying him, he might now add *shrew* to the list of other charming attributes he had for her, but so be it. 'I'm not nagging you, but if you insist on acting like a little boy, then that's exactly how I'm going to treat you!' It was worth it to watch the expression of disbelief on his face as he stared at her. Women didn't nag him, didn't chivvy him, and certainly never told him that he was acting like a child!

'I don't suppose I can stop you from trying to get some work done, but I'll just tell you that, the more work you do now, the less capable you'll be of getting out of bed in the morning. Lord knows, I'm surprised your body's taken this long to tell you that it needs a break!'

'Have you ever considered a career as a matron?' Rafe finally rediscovered the power of speech. 'Or perhaps something in the prison service?' Curiously, her bossiness, which was quite frankly the least feminine trait he could think of, didn't ruffle his feathers. He stood up and belted the robe. 'Bring up those documents Patricia sent over with you. I think my raging fever can accommodate a *little* work.' He paused in front of her and smiled slowly. 'You do that sergeant-major impersonation very well, did you know that?'

'And you do the offensive patient very well, did you know that?'

She could hear him chuckling softly as she whipped round the room, scooping up her bag, the papers and of course his laptop computer, which she doubted he could exist without for longer than a few minutes.

Matron? Prison officer? Sergeant-major? Her cheeks were burning as she sprinted up behind him, to see him disappearing through one of the doors.

This wasn't even supposed to be part of her job! Yes, she was supposed to follow him, to shadow his movements so that she could write a comprehensive piece about him, but playing nursemaid? Dashing in the rain to the shops to fetch him some cold and flu medicine?

She pelted through the open door, still fuming, and stopped dead in her tracks.

It was a big bedroom. Enormous. Two wood-panelled walls gave it a feeling of mellow warmth, as did the dark furniture and the masculine colours of deep reds and blues. The bed was unmade, with the sheets and pillows and quilt chaotically rumpled. And in the middle of his room, there he was, standing with his back to her, his body no longer even sparingly partially concealed by the robe, which had been discarded, joining the tangled linen on the bed.

Sophie had the disorienting feeling of everything slowing down for a few seconds, only to accelerate until the room seemed to be spinning around her at top speed.

At least he had had the decency to keep his boxer shorts on, but not even these provided a safe haven for her eyes because they just accentuated the perfection of his body, the broadness of his shoulders tapering down to his waist, the powerful length of his legs.

Sophie gulped, eyes wide. She must have made a noise as well, because to her horror he turned around and faced her, making no attempt to cover himself.

'Good. You brought my things up.' He walked towards her and she fell back a couple of inches, clutching the laptop and papers to her chest like a protective shield.

His body was almost indecently masculine. Fine, dark hairs on his chest, stomach hard and flat, shoulders rippling lightly with muscles as he moved. She looked away and cleared her throat.

'Do you mind…getting changed, Rafe?'

Rafe halted in mid-stride. 'You're not *embarrassed*, are you, Sophie? I was about to climb into bed, in actual fact. You know, you can look at me. I'm not completely naked.'

He knew that this was a childish ploy. He had timed removal of the robe with exquisite precision because he had guessed just what her reaction would be and she was not disappointing him. She looked as though she was issuing a silent but heartfelt prayer to the gods to rescue her from her situation. And if she held onto that laptop computer any harder, she would have a job flexing the muscles in her fingers afterwards.

He could only think that it was the intense boredom of finding himself cooped up against his will that had encouraged this uncharacteristically juvenile gambit. That and the desire to enjoy the delicate bloom on her cheeks, the flitting of emotion across her face that he had recently found himself rather drawn to.

The devil and idle hands, he supposed.

With a little sigh, he headed towards the bed, slipped

under the covers and watched as she tried to gather her scattered wits sufficiently to approach him.

'You would see the same on any beach,' he pointed out reasonably. 'If I embarrassed you, I apologise. You were right, anyway. Better to be up here, much as I hate to admit it.'

Sophie risked glancing over. 'Aren't you going to put on any…pyjamas?'

'Don't possess any. Not all of us do.' He grinned innocently at her, just enough to make her realise that he knew precisely where that observation was leading, right to her bedroom and his gentlemanly changing of her clothes. Sophie chose to ignore him.

She deposited the computer on his bed, along with the documents Patricia had given her, and stepped back. She was finding it increasingly unnerving being here, being in his house, his bedroom. He was bored and it was a dangerous situation for a man who operated continually in fifth gear.

There had been no need for him to get undressed when he had known that she was following him up the stairs.

'Is there anything else you want?' she asked, and then quickly rephrased the question. 'I mean, I really should be heading back now, but I can bring you up some water…you'll need to take more of that medicine in about four hours' time…'

'Food,' Rafe told her succinctly, switching on his computer and frowning at the screen.

'I beg your pardon?'

'You asked me if there was anything I wanted. Food. I haven't eaten this morning.'

'You want *food*?' Sophie gaped.

'Starve a cold and all that.' He glanced up at her from

his computer. 'Why? Is it too much trouble for you? Your job is to be with me at all times, isn't it?'

'Yes, but...'

'I'm not asking you to do anything extraordinary. Just some eggs and toast, perhaps...'

'Cooking for you wasn't really part of my assignment,' she said stoutly.

'I'm ill. I have a raging fever. You said so yourself. It seems we tycoons do fall prey to things beyond our control. That's an interesting aspect you could cover in your article. The *human touch* you're so keen to incorporate...'

'You haven't got a raging fever!' But his attention was already back with whatever was on his computer screen and, with a muffled snort, Sophie found herself heading off towards the kitchen and wondering how she had managed to find herself in this position.

There had to be something she gave off, some scent, that alerted people to that side of her that was the home-bird. Whenever one of her friends had been poorly in the past, she had always been the one they called, the one who came round with the shopping and made them cups of tea. That was fine for friends, she thought sourly, but when it came to Rafael Loro, it smacked of being used.

The kitchen, through the dining area and overlooking the back garden, turned out to be an interesting mixture of homely furniture—a lovely, worn pine table, chairs, old mat in front of an Aga—and state-of-the-art appliances. It took several minutes to locate what she needed, several more to work out the toaster and the coffee machine, and a good half an hour before she was wending her way back up the stairs to his bedroom, with scrambled eggs on toast, juice and coffee all laid out on a tray, along with cutlery and a napkin.

And he still hadn't dressed. He was sitting up in bed, the

quilt loosely draped over his lower half, leaving his upper half exposed and not even partially hidden by his computer, which he had thoughtfully shoved to the side in expectation of the tray on his lap.

Feeling like room service, Sophie sourly placed the tray on the chest of drawers and, ignoring his questions, rummaged in one of the drawers until she came up with a tee shirt, a dark green tee shirt with an expensive logo on the front pocket, which she tossed over at him.

'You wouldn't want to compound your cold with third-degree burns from spilling hot coffee on yourself, would you?' she asked sweetly. Rafe grinned and obediently stuck on the tee shirt.

'Better?'

'Here's your order.' Sophie placed the tray squarely on his lap and stood back while he made appreciative noises under his breath.

'Smells good. I can spot a domestic goddess a mile off.' He dug into his food with an enthusiasm that pointed to some very hungry germs. Sophie wondered whether he was as ill as he was making out and came to the conclusion that, like most men, he was just making a mountain out of a molehill. It was more understandable considering he had no real recognition of the average virus, having never been visited by one.

'Sit down,' he commanded, concentrating on his eggs and toast. 'You're making me uncomfortable standing there with your arms folded.'

'Oh, I was just trying to conform to my sergeant-major image,' Sophie informed him. She could have kicked herself for the little outburst which, rather than sounding coldly sarcastic as intended, emerged as a petulant, childish complaint. 'Patricia was worried about you,' she carried on.

'Would you like me to telephone her just to let her know that you're all right?'

'If I was all right, I would be at work,' Rafe said irritably. 'That tasted great. You can cook my eggs any time you want.'

Sophie went to recover the tray, waiting as he removed his coffee-cup. 'Thanks, but I'll pass on that offer.'

For some reason Rafe felt unaccountably annoyed with the remark. As annoyed as he felt watching her as she busied herself trying to juggle the tray in one hand and hang onto her bag with the other.

'For God's sake, sit down, will you? I doubt taking a few minutes out of your carefully planned day is going to hurt!'

Sophie was so startled at the sharpness of the demand that she actually obeyed him. She sat. On the bed next to him, tray on her lap, handbag at her feet.

'Okay, so it might not be part of the master plan to have found yourself here, but, now that you have, why don't you accept the situation and make the most of it? After all,' he added slyly, 'you find me a captive audience.'

'All right.' She felt him shift his legs slightly under the quilt and licked her lips. 'Here's a question: why did you ask me to come over? I mean, why *me*? If you wanted someone to fetch you some cold capsules and cook you breakfast, wouldn't the obvious option have been Angela? I mean, how is she going to feel, knowing that I'm here with you? Or you could have asked Patricia to come over with the documents…'

'I suppose I could have asked Patricia to come over, but, no…that would not have worked.' He folded his arms behind his head. 'We have amicable but rigid lines established between us. She would have been highly uncomfortable being here, in my house, seeing me as an invalid…'

'Oh, good grief. Anyone would think you were suffering from something serious! What about Angela, then?'

The lazy smile dropped off his face immediately and he frowned. 'Oh, no. That wouldn't have worked at all.'

'Why?' Sophie could think of nothing nicer than being taken care of by your partner, knowing that every solicitous action came from love and affection and a real desire to help. Her face softened.

'For the same reason your eyes seem to have misted over,' Rafe said dryly. 'Angela would have liked nothing better than to swan around my house, sticking on a housewife hat and patting my fevered brow. Her cooking skills might have been open to question, but she would have relished the prospect of having a go.'

'And you wouldn't have wanted to encourage that.'

'Very sharp of you, my dear Watson. Besides, her secretarial skills are atrocious and I want you to do some letters for me…'

Which took them until lunchtime. By which point, he had at least moved operations back down to the sitting room and had clothed himself in something a little less alarming than a bathrobe. The letters, optimistically promised to take no longer than an hour, at the tops, turned into corrections to several reports, interrupted by phone calls that Rafe insisted on taking despite complaints about a sore throat.

At one, as the phone rang yet again Sophie held up her hand and stopped him from picking up the receiver.

'Leave it to me,' she said. At this rate, she would be lucky to leave by nightfall, and she had to. Not only did she have her own work to do, including reporting back to her company on how her assignment was coming along, but she was uneasily aware that she was enjoying being in his company. This was a side to him she hadn't glimpsed before, with an edge of vulnerability that was endearing.

Sophie didn't want endearing. Endearing might make successful copy, but it did nothing for her equilibrium.

She had expected another wretched client, none of whom seemed able to survive without making contact with the big boss himself, and had worked out a strategy for making sure that the phone call was terminated before it could generate another spate of letters. Instead, she heard the distinctive voice of Claudia Loro.

As luck would have it, Claudia recognised her voice instantly and with a silent groan of dismay she could tell, from that initial, fractional pause, that the older woman was wondering what her friend's daughter was doing in Rafe's house.

And, Claudia being Claudia, she made no attempt to beat about the bush. She asked directly and with interest. And waited for an answer.

'I'm...' Sophie looked desperately over to Rafe and mouthed: *It's your mother*. His returning grin did nothing for her growing sense of frustration. 'I'm...just here... doing my job...'

'In his *house*? How very thorough of you, darling!'

'No! I mean...I did go to work this morning, as usual, but Rafe isn't awfully well at the moment and...'

'You decided to go and take care of him!' Claudia sounded delighted. 'I take it it's nothing serious or I would have heard. Probably just a common cold. You know men, though—such babies.'

Sophie looked across at Rafe and smirked. 'Yes, he's really such a baby,' she agreed wholeheartedly. 'Moaning and pleading for painkillers every two minutes.'

'But it was sweet of you to rush to his bedside.' Claudia's voice was thoughtful.

'Oh, I didn't rush! In fact, I was ordered to come across. Rafe wanted some documents...'

'Oh, really? I would have thought that any decent courier service would have been able to deliver—not that the personal touch isn't much better, my dear. It is! And I expect he's had you cooking for him as well...?'

'Not *cooking* as such, no. Just some scrambled egg, but actually I was about to leave when you called. How's Mum? Tell her I'm sorry I haven't called for a few days, if you see her, and I promise I'll be in touch later tonight. Shall I put you onto your son? He apparently has a sore throat, although he doesn't seem to have lost use of his voice.' She handed the phone to Rafe and remained standing, hoping that he would simply wave her away while he continued chatting to his mother on the telephone. He didn't. He obviously saw no need for privacy when it came to talking to his mother, and she could understand why, since most of the talking seemed to be done by her. Rafe responded largely in monosyllables. An avid eavesdropper would have been unable to glean a thing from the grunting, noncommittal nature of his responses. For all she could tell, he could have been conducting a conversation with someone in a foreign language.

'I must go,' Sophie said as soon as he was off the phone. 'Is there anything else you want me to fetch for you before I leave?'

'Have you noticed how mothers have a unique ability to inspire guilt?' Rafe looked at her in wry amusement and Sophie was distracted enough to return his amusement.

'Always,' she agreed. She was already feeling guilty at her own negligence in phoning her mother and predicting her mother's remarks, or pointed lack of them, when she did get round to calling later. Her mother always adopted a casual approach, proclaiming abhorrence for these children who left home only to feel a duty to clock in at pre-arranged times during the week, but it wasn't hard for Sophie to hear the anxiety whenever she missed a couple of days. It was oddly endearing.

'Apparently my responsibility was to telephone the very second the thought occurred to me that I might be going down with something.'

'I'm surprised Claudia didn't offer to come down and look after you.'

'Oh, she did, but I told her that I was in good hands...'

'You didn't!' No, of course he hadn't, she would have heard him. She'd been right there in the room! He hadn't said anything as provocative as that.

'Don't tell me you find another implied insult in that remark,' Rafe said mildly. Of course she didn't. It was simply the unspoken, and for her probably unconscious, nebulous recognition that his mother would be adept at drawing conclusions where none should be drawn. He himself had had no difficulty in spotting Claudia's rapid assessment of Sophie being in his house, looking after him, a man who had never asked any woman to look after him in his life before.

He would normally have been angry at the assumption, but...

Rafe looked lazily at Sophie from under half-closed eyes. She was frowning slightly. He had fast become accustomed to that small frown. It usually heralded one of her outspoken outbursts, as though contemplating the passage of her thoughts was just a formality before her mouth said precisely what it wanted to.

He hadn't expected it to happen, but happen it had. She had moved from being an irritation to an itch that he felt compelled to scratch.

'My mother has invited us to the Cornwall flat for the

weekend,' Rafe drawled into the growing silence. 'Apparently your mother will be there as well, along with two other bridge-playing cronies. She seems to think some bracing coastal air will do me good…and on behalf of both of us, I've accepted.'

CHAPTER SIX

THIS was a nightmare idea.

Sophie stared into the mirror at her reflection, in no mood to appreciate the dramatic scenery outside, shrouded though it was in darkness at nine-thirty on a Friday evening.

Against her better judgement and caught like a worm on a hook, she had allowed herself to be persuaded into going down to Cornwall thanks to the joint efforts of her mother, who had skirted softly but meaningfully around the bald truth that she missed seeing her daughter, Claudia, who had simply declared it to be a splendid idea and allowed no room for manoeuvre, and Rafe, who for reasons unknown seemed to follow his mother's unlikely line of thought.

And now here she was.

Pleading things to do, she had managed to wriggle out of the drive down with Rafe, taking the train instead, but there had been no opportunity to wriggle anywhere once she had arrived.

She had been greeted like the prodigal son by her mother and Claudia and even the two old biddies, both of whom she knew from the village. Rafe, who seemed to have recovered doubly fortified after his brush with the common cold, watched from an amused distance, but she was all too aware of him standing there, hands shoved into his pockets, leaning indolently against the wall.

In the presence of Claudia and her mother, she had felt like the teenager she had once been, horribly aware of Rafe with his dangerous masculine sex appeal, sensitive to every word uttered in that deep, velvety voice. The conversation over dinner had been light-hearted and easy, but she had still been aware of him, sitting next to her, passing her the vegetables, his fingers accidentally brushing hers every so often, his thigh only inches away from hers so that she felt compelled to squeeze her legs shut just in case... And there was no Work Talk to cover up the cracks in her composure. Her mother and Grace had dutifully spent a few minutes showing an interest in how the assignment was going, but then they expected both her and Rafe to simply enjoy the weekend for what it was, and that entailed not mentioning work at all. Rafe appeared to have no problem with that. In fact, it would have been a job to spot the ruthless workaholic beneath the casual, relaxed charmer. She, on the other hand, was left miserably wondering where her easygoing personality had gone.

When the four ladies had retired for coffee and bridge, she had felt a physical release of tension that she could escape up to her bedroom and ponder the horrifying realisation that she was stupidly, dangerously attracted to Rafael Loro.

How she had managed to kid herself otherwise was beyond her comprehension.

Shouldn't it have made perfect sense from the very beginning? The way he made her nervous? The way her eyes flicked across at him whenever she imagined he wasn't looking? The way she felt energised and *alive* in his company even when she was arguing with him and telling herself that she really, truly disliked him?

The way, she thought now, her body had felt when she had seen him wearing only his bathrobe? As if it had been on fire.

And, as if all that weren't bad enough, she had had to contend with the thinly veiled looks of conspiracy that had darted between Claudia and her mother. Thinly veiled, *smug* looks of conspiracy.

She had had her bath and ostensibly retired for the night over an hour ago, pleading exhaustion with the handy additional excuse of maybe *coming down with something* to add substance to her excuse.

Now, on the spur of the moment, she decided to pay Rafe a little visit. If she had noticed those looks, then he most certainly would have as well. And the thought of having him think that their parents were somehow trying to push them together made her cringe in horror. What if he thought that she was somehow behind it? Had maybe confided an attraction to him to her mother in some girlish chat down the telephone, had encouraged them to think that they could somehow manoeuvre him into an unlikely romance? After all, hadn't she been the girl who had once looked at him with adoring sheep's eyes?

Starting from point A, her mind travelled to point Z with remorseless speed. Along the way it picked up sufficient sickening scenarios to have her hands trembling with urgency as she flung on a pair of jeans and a tee shirt and made her way down to the sitting room, which was where he would be, leaving the kitchen free for the four women to play their bridge.

She knew the layout of the house from memory, even though it had been years since she had last visited it. When her father had been alive, in fact, which would have made her just barely into her teens at the time. It was one of those charming little whitewashed cottages, halfway up a narrow street that tumbled down towards the harbour. Deceptively small on the outside, but with a honeycomb of rooms, a fair few of which had splendid views across the sea.

She knew to avoid the kitchen, although she could hear

the sounds of laughter and chatting that always accompanied Claudia's bridge parties. Serious playing of cards was almost a sin as far as she was concerned. Bids were made in between general gossip and jokes, and rubbers won over an interminable array of snacks and glasses of wine or cups of tea, depending on the time of day.

Despite the ancient appearance of the cottage, there was no shortage of modernisation inside, including comprehensive central heating, which was turned on to the fullest. She could, she knew, have comfortably walked around barefoot on the wooden floors, but had chosen to slip on her bedroom slippers.

Thus, her feet made very little sound as she headed directly towards the sitting room. Like all the other rooms in the house, it was small but exquisite. Claudia had impeccable taste and had lavished the utmost care in decorating the cottage. As investments went, it had been a brilliant buy all those years ago before Cornwall had become popular with the rich and the beautiful.

It was just a shame that it never received the level of use it should have. She doubted Rafe ever visited or, if he did, it would only have been under duress.

She paused by the door to the sitting room and looked, for a few unseen seconds, at the object of her thoughts.

Rafe was sitting in front of the fire, his profile to her, long legs stretched out, head flung back and eyes closed. Sophie's system went into sudden freefall and she had to breathe deeply to steady herself, then she knocked lightly and walked in, not giving herself time to chicken out and scuttle back up to the safety of her bedroom.

He opened his eyes and half turned towards her.

How was it possible for a man to look so sexy in such ordinary clothes? He was just wearing a pair of old, faded grey chinos and an ancient rugby shirt that was probably a legacy from his rugby-playing university days, but he still managed to be a knockout.

'I thought you had retired for the night?' he drawled, not shifting, just watching with hooded eyes as she moved to sit on the other chair by the fire. 'Seduced by the glamour of a cup of hot chocolate and a good book?'

Sophie blushed. 'I just thought it might be tactful to leave you to get on with some work, and I could hardly stay in the kitchen and have my hot chocolate.'

'As you can see, I haven't exactly been getting very much done.' He reached forward and tossed a couple of logs into the open fire, which was beginning to die. Immediately, there was a comforting sizzle and it regained strength, bringing a sudden blast of heat into the room. Rafe shoved up the sleeves of his rugby shirt and relaxed back into the deep chair. 'Do you think having one day off work has set me down the wrong road?' he asked with lazy interest. What he didn't tell her was that it felt damned good to take some time out, some *unexpected* time out. A first, for him. He was beginning to think that there hadn't been too many firsts in his life recently. Everything always according to plan, every angle of his life utterly in control, even his women.

'Oh, absolutely,' Sophie said with a straight face. 'You wouldn't want to go mad and start thinking that there's a life out there that doesn't involve running an empire.'

Rafe laughed softly, not taking his eyes off her, and she felt a tingle run up and down her spine. This, she thought nervously, was seductive, not some hot drink and a good book.

'You have a good sense of humour. Anyone ever told you that? Dry. Not very obvious.'

Sophie ignored the warning bells that started ringing in her head. He wasn't flirting, she told herself, he was *chat-*

ting. It was only the combination of being in Cornwall, with the sound of the sea breeze whipping against the windows, and the timbre of his voice, that made it sound like flirting.

And probably her own hypersensitivity as well, just her newly attuned antennae picking up wavelengths that weren't there, making her jumpy, filling her with hot, shameful excitement.

'My sense of humour is perfectly ordinary,' she heard herself say, in a very prissy voice. 'Maybe you just don't have much experience going out with women who have a sense of humour at all.'

'Tut-tut. Very catty. Was that a dig at Angela, by any chance?'

Sophie went red. 'It was a general observation. I don't know Angela, so how would I be able to have a dig at her? I'm sure she's a perfectly nice woman.'

'Just not very funny.'

Sophie looked at the fire and didn't answer.

'Come on, Sophie. You can speak your mind. After all, I'm not the one dissecting you so that I can produce a human interest story.'

'I'm not dissecting you!' Her eyes flashed at him to see that his were spiced with laughter and she smiled reluctantly back at him. 'You're doing it again,' she said ruefully. 'Distracting me.'

'Now, there's an admission.'

'I meant that I came in here to have a talk to you about…' She felt hot under the collar. Worse, she wondered how she was going to raise the subject of their respective mothers and those *little looks* without losing the plot somewhere along the way. When he was looking at her like that. There was no overhead light on, just the dull gleam from two table lamps, but it was still enough for her to make out the disconcerting, intimate expression on his face. Did he even know the effect he was having on her?

'But now that you mention Angela,' she said, in an effort to remind him of his girlfriend and bring the conversation back down to earth, 'how is she?'

'I have no idea. I'm afraid I had to terminate that relationship. Yesterday, as a matter of fact.'

Sophie looked at him in surprise.

'There's no need to look so shocked,' Rafe said irritably. 'We were never heading for a walk down the aisle.'

'Yes, but she seemed so keen on you. Poor woman.'

'Why *poor woman*? I doubt she'll have much trouble finding my replacement.' The unspoken criticism on her face had brought the atmosphere between them to a grinding halt. And she called *him* a distraction! 'I was doing her a favour,' he expanded, wondering why he was bothering to justify perfectly reasonable behaviour. 'The longer she stayed in the relationship, the more she might have started nurturing ideas of permanency.'

'I'm bowled over by your logic,' Sophie told him.

Nothing amusing in that particular dry statement, Rafe thought with exasperation. What century was she living in? 'And to be blunt, I would have driven her crazy within weeks. I doubt there's a woman on the face of the earth who would find my work schedule acceptable.'

'You're probably right,' Sophie agreed, which actually just made him more exasperated. He opened his mouth to continue the debate and then had second thoughts. Where would it lead?

'You were saying that you came in here to talk to me. What about? I gather it wasn't simply general chit-chat.'

'Actually, it was about…well, Mum and Claudia.'

Rafe looked at Sophie, astonished. 'What about them?'

'Well, how did they seem to you?'

'Much the same as usual.' Rafe frowned. 'The usual gossip about who was seen where and why and who's suffering from what new ailment, and the headache of the spring bazaar, which Mother, bizarrely, has volunteered to have on the grounds of the house and is now regretting…nothing spectacular there. Why?'

'I just wondered.'

'No, you didn't *just wonder*.' He took in the embarrassed confusion on her face and was suddenly intrigued. Sophie Frey, he had discovered, did not aimlessly make statements. With any other woman, a provocative remark always, but always, was destined to lead to generating a response in him, capturing his interest, continuing the game of chase that sophisticated adults seemed to enjoy playing. That *he* had always enjoyed playing.

'All right,' Sophie said on a sigh. 'I don't know how to explain it, but I think you ought to have a word to your mother about us…I mean, just put her on the right track…'

'I have no idea what you're talking about,' Rafe said, leaning forward, elbows resting on his thighs, thoroughly intrigued now.

'Oh, don't be so dense, Rafe. You must have noticed those little looks they kept giving one another all evening, glancing at us and then glancing at each other as though…as though…'

'Ah.' He sat back with a slow smile. 'Now that you mention it, I did notice something a little conniving about their attitude. In fact, come to think of it, there were a few questions about how we were getting along and how wonderful it was that we were both coming to Cornwall to visit…' Gentleman as he was, Rafe decided to allow Sophie the chance to carry on with this particular line of thought.

'And what did you tell them?'

'Oh, that we were getting along famously.'

'Which isn't true!' Sophie cried. 'You hate the fact that I'm cluttering up your day, you resent it when I ask questions, and did you happen to mention that now you've decided that you're lumbered with an emotional liability who obviously can't take care of herself in case she's pounced on by some unscrupulous man on the lookout for an easy lay?'

'Don't call yourself that!' he said sharply. 'That kind of language doesn't suit you!'

'You should have been blunt with them. You know what they're like! Now they're thinking that…that there's something between us. I can read it on their faces!' The words were out and it all sounded ridiculous. She looked down at her hands and smoothed them over her thighs, calming herself. Even if he wanted to roar with laughter, at least now he was warned that, whatever her mother and Claudia were hinting at, it had nothing to do with *her*.

'It's crazy,' she said steadily. 'My mother knows that you are the last kind of man I would ever be interested in, just as your mother must know that you're attracted to…well…to women like Angela…'

'Perhaps she aspires to a different sort of woman for me…' Rafe murmured softly.

Sophie licked her dry lips. His face was all angles and shadows and so, so compelling. She stood up, desperate to escape feelings running rampant inside her. 'That's as maybe,' she said, summoning up the skills of an award-winning actress to sound matter-of-fact and brisk, 'but you'll just have to disabuse her on that count.'

'Why?'

The single word dropped like a stone into still water, sending ripples outwards. Sophie's eyes widened and she watched, mesmerised, as he stood up and strolled the few paces over to where she was sitting, pushing back into the chair. He leant over, propping himself up on the arms of the chair, caging her in.

'B-because…' she stuttered.

'Because none of it is true? Because I'm not attracted to you in the slightest? Because you don't feel a thing for me?' He allowed his devastating questions to have their effect.

'Of course!'

'So sure about that?' He trailed his finger along her cheek and the sudden catapulting rush of sensation nearly knocked him off his feet. 'Because I'm not…'

Sophie froze. There was a weird, dreamlike quality about what was happening that made her think that if she exhaled or blinked it would disappear in a puff of smoke. She would wake up from a restless dream and everything would have slotted back into normality. She exhaled, blinked and he was still there, and his finger was still sending red hot tingles through her.

'Don't be absurd!' she stammered, turning her head away, and he rested his finger on her chin and inexorably guided her face until she was once more looking at him.

'I'm not being absurd, Sophie. I'm being realistic. Why hide from it? Tell me that you're not in the slightest attracted to me and I'll walk away right now and you can pretend that none of this has ever happened.' Except, of course, he wouldn't. He knew that. This was just one of those firsts he had been contemplating and he wanted her. He wanted the challenge of her. His desire was so powerful that he could feel it like hot lava, burning through his veins. It was irresistible.

Sophie opened her mouth to speak and nothing came out. In that silent fraction of a second, she knew that he was going to kiss her and, with a small sigh of helpless, wanton, treacherous surrender, she closed her eyes and gave herself up to the touch of his lips against hers, gentle at first and then hungrily insistent, exploring her mouth, tongue against tongue.

She groaned and then reached up to wind her hands around his neck, arching up so that she could savour the exquisite taste of his mouth. Her heart was beating like a drum inside her and her body was reacting in ways she had never experienced before. Her breasts physically ached and she knew that she was damp between her legs, soft and moist and ready.

If his hands untwined themselves from her hair and ventured anywhere else, she just knew that she would explode and, Lord, she didn't want it to stop. Only she did. When Claudia's voice reached them, getting closer.

With a silent curse, Rafe stood up, his aroused hardness still pulsating.

He moved swiftly towards the door, forestalling his mother, and Sophie, horrified, began straightening herself. Her hands were trembling and her nipples were hard and pushing against her tee shirt.

'What on earth are you two children doing in here?' she heard Claudia asking interestedly, and Sophie immediately sprang out of the chair and headed towards the door.

'Working!' She walked around Rafe and folded her arms. If her grin smile got any wider, her face would crack.

'Working? At this hour?'

'Well, actually…' Rafe began and Sophie interrupted him swiftly.

'I thought it might be a good idea to let Rafe have a look at what I've done so far. The assignment, you know? He's hardly ever in one place at the office! And, really, I haven't got much longer to tie things up, so I need to find out whether there are any bits of it that he wants editing out.'

'Of course, darling.' Claudia's face dropped ever so slightly. 'Well, I didn't mean to disturb you, but—'

'You're not disturbing us at all!' Sophie interrupted brightly. 'In fact, I was just on my way out.'

'I wanted to know about tomorrow, what plans you two may have.' Claudia got back into her usual stride. 'Which I *hope* doesn't include more work! You're here to have a well-deserved rest!' This to her son. 'The four of us are thinking about getting an early start and heading into the town, probably stay there for a spot of lunch, weather permitting. Now, would you two like to join us?'

This time it was Rafe's turn to answer and his reply was so swift and smooth that it barely gave Sophie time for her brain to get into gear. She just heard him turning down the offer, telling his mother that they would do their own thing and that, no, he could solemnly promise that work would not intrude. At all.

Which appeared to satisfy Claudia. It didn't satisfy Sophie. She turned to him furiously as soon as his mother had disappeared back to the kitchen, where it seemed the night birds were contemplating their beds.

'Why did you say that?'

'My mother interrupted us. I hate being interrupted. I hate having unfinished business.'

'I am *not* unfinished business!'

'Maybe not. In which case we can always join them for their little spree, although I'll bet you the last thing any of them wants is the two of us trekking along behind them.' He paused. 'Anyway, I really *would* be interested in reading what you've written so far. After all, the condemned man has to have a chance to put across his point of view…'

'Nothing would go to print unless you'd given it the

okay,' Sophie said. 'I haven't brought the proper copy with me, just my file with notes in it.' She struggled to find the right words to bring the conversation back to his disturbing remark about *unfinished business*, and Rafe, reading her mind, decided to help her out.

'And to set your mind at rest, I'll be the perfect gentleman.' He took in her unruly hair, her suspicious face, and dropped his eyes. She was waiting to attack him, but she was on uncertain ground. He certainly hadn't taken advantage of her. She had been as enthusiastic about kissing him as he had been about kissing her. It had been a mutual abandonment every inch of the way. And it had left him wanting more, much, much more, but steaming in like a horny rhino would have her running as fast as her legs could take her and he didn't want her running, not unless it was in his direction.

'Or we could take up my mother's invitation to trawl through the town in a cosy six-some,' he offered with a shrug. 'Tea at ten, conversations about the spring fête...' He gave her an innocent, perfectly dry smile.

'I'll show you my notes and run through them with you, and then, if you don't mind, I'd quite like to make my own way into town. There are one or two things I wouldn't mind getting.'

'Fair deal. I have work to do here anyway. I could use the peace before everyone gets back from their day trip.'

Sophie was barely aware of what to expect the following morning. She had spent the night restlessly pouring over what had happened. He had kissed her and she had melted. It was as simple as that. She wasn't a fool. She knew that he was vastly experienced when it came to the opposite sex, that the way he had made her feel had required next to no effort from him. She also knew that none of it should have happened, but what was the use in trying to shut the stable door after the horse had bolted? She could beat herself up over it or she could endure the weekend as best she could, knowing that she just had to write up her assignment and then she would be out of his office and out of his life for ever.

There was also no point in dwelling obsessively on what he had said—that he was attracted to her. It didn't *mean* anything. He must have said those words a million times to a thousand different women. Her job wasn't to analyse his motivations; her job was to protect herself because she knew how dangerous he could be for her, how easy it would be to let him in through that tiny crack that he had already managed to spot.

The first step in protecting herself was to make sure she dressed as sexlessly as possible.

Jeans, faded, sensible brogues for the aimless walk she had ahead of her when their work chat was over, thick, ribbed polo-necked jumper in an eminently sensible colour, brown, hair tied back into two plaits, because no one could ever convince her that a man who made it his duty to escort some of the most beautiful women in the country would look twice at a girl wearing plaits. Never mind all that talk about being attracted to her.

Sophie looked at herself in the mirror and snorted derisively. With cold daylight streaming through the windows, it was much easier to get the whole thing into perspective. In the dead of night, it had been another matter. Then, yes, she had heard his dark, velvety voice whispering, turning her on, had felt her body grow hot with yearning, had even touched herself, hoping to quench the fire inside her...

She shuddered and stood up, briskly tidying up the room and straightening the bed. Then she fetched her file from her overnight bag and headed downstairs. At a little after nine, she was unsurprised to find that the women had all departed for the day and even more unsurprised to find Rafe up, alert and halfway through a pot of coffee, with the newspapers in front of him and his mobile phone on the kitchen table.

He turned to her as soon as she walked into the kitchen and Sophie's heart skipped a beat. He was in some grey trousers and a black jumper and he had dragged one of the kitchen chairs into a strategic position as a foot rest. The workaholic at leisure, she told herself, closing her mind to his suffocating sex appeal. *Financial Times* and cell phone within easy reach.

And, true to his word, he was being the perfect gentleman as he offered her breakfast, which she refused, and coffee, which she accepted. The night before might never have happened. She had expected some reference to it, in that cryptic way he had, but nothing. Sophie didn't know whether to feel relieved or disappointed, then decided that she was definitely relieved.

'What time did they all leave?' Sophie asked politely, sipping the coffee and watching him over the rim of her cup.

'Only about ten minutes ago. I offered to drive them in, but they seemed to prefer the excitement of going in Edith Bailey's ageing car. Something about being free to do their own thing.' He could continue in this vein till the cows came home, and would do if necessary. Talking about nothing, circling each other while the tension built between them. This was certainly a game he had never played before. He realised, with mild surprise, that serious chasing of any woman had never really featured in his life. He chased, but they both knew the game from the start and where it would lead. With this woman…he thought she would punch him on the jaw if he tried to speed things up a little.

They chatted about nothing in particular for the duration of the coffee, then he moved into second gear and asked to see her file.

'You won't understand my shorthand,' Sophie told him. 'But I'll run through it with you.' She opened up the file, all business now. 'I intend to concentrate largely on what put you on the map, in other words a bit about your background and your university education. Also I'll list all your corporate successes—'

'What about my corporate failures?'

'Have you had any of those?' Her extensive research had not thrown up any.

'No.' He grinned at her. 'None to date.'

The change in atmosphere was so swift and so subtle that Sophie almost wondered whether she had imagined it, because when she glanced up at him his face was once more blandly interested.

'Right...so if I read you what I have...' She skimmed over the bones of the report, making sure that she had got the facts right. 'Then, I shall devote a bit to making you more human. You crop up in gossip columns now and again with different women on your arm, but I intend to humanise you, portray you as someone who plays hard and works hard, but basically is still prey to the desires we all share.'

'Which might be what?'

'A desire to make sure that you do your best for your mother, that your work is at least partially motivated by the pride you take from furthering your father's businesses, et cetera, et cetera. Obviously there are casualties on the way to the top.' She looked at him seriously. 'The little people who suffer as a result of some of your takeovers...'

'Details of deals are unacceptable, Sophie. Those are private and confidential. If you want to run a report on the little people who have suffered, then you can do so separately, but bear in mind that most of those so-called *little people* have gained quite a bit in the process. I thought we had gone past my stereotype as the heartless monster.'

'I'm not saying that you're a heartless monster, Rafe. Simply that you are typical of someone who's made it to the very top. You don't achieve that by being kind and thoughtful. You achieve it by being ruthless and prepared to deal with anyone who threatens to scupper your plans as efficiently as possible.'

'Not a very attractive trait,' Rafe said coldly.

'Perhaps you aren't a very attractive person.' Sophie felt her heart begin to race. It had been a crashingly provocative statement, but, in all events, he chose to ignore it, asking her to move on.

'I also intend to refer in a bit more detail about your reputation with women.' She waited for him to challenge her on that, but he didn't. 'People like reading about the rich and famous, about how they live and where they live and what they wear, and, in the case of someone like you, young, powerful, single, attractive, they like reading about your love life. It makes good copy.'

'And what do you intend to write?'

'You know what I intend to write, Rafe. It's nothing you could possibly disagree with. Naturally, I won't name names and I'll do my utmost not to make you sound like a—a reprobate.'

'Good of you.'

His eyes were unreadable and Sophie faltered on for a few seconds before grinding to an awkward halt. 'That's about all,' she said lamely. 'I still have to fine-tune a couple of things, and then I'll have it ready for you to read by the end of next week.' She stood up. 'If you don't mind, I think

I'll go and have a little walk now. Down to the harbour. Let you get on with your work.'

She wished he would say something, but he just looked at her and nodded, and Sophie miserably went upstairs. He couldn't wait to get rid of her, to the point where he no longer had the energy to argue with what she said. She rested the file on the dressing table and began rummaging in her suitcase for her scarf and gloves. It was a bright day, but freezing. Walking outside would do her good, because right now her head was spinning with a hornet's nest of painful assumptions.

She had followed him around, had seen all his downsides, and yet she had still let herself be seduced. He had kissed her and her world had fragmented into a thousand little pieces and she had only herself to blame.

Now, he couldn't wait to get rid of her fast enough. He had kissed her and, no doubt, he would have followed that up with the whole seduction process if the time and place had been any different, and if she had fallen into his arms and begged him to continue. But she had pulled away and, really, why should he bother with someone pulling away from him? Whatever he said? His ocean was full of fish. Why go for the one that didn't immediately seize the bait?

She located the errant scarf and wrapped it around her, still squatting in front of her open bag and letting her thoughts run wild. Perversely enjoying it, too. What was the point of making a complete fool of yourself if you didn't do it in grand style? she thought bitterly. It made her teenage infatuation look like a walk in the park. She slammed shut the bag and was straightening up, her joints creaking from sitting back on her heels for too long, when he spoke from the doorway behind her.

'Bit rich, isn't it? Turning me into a predator?'

Her head swung round and she saw him leaning against

the doorframe, face grimly unsmiling. 'When you of all people should know that I would never pursue a woman and make her do anything against her will...or are you too cowardly to face that simple truth?'

'You should be working.' Sophie gasped, staring up at him from the floor.

He took a couple of steps into the room and shut the door behind him. 'Time for me to compile my report on *you*, Sophie Frey. And you'll listen, whether you like it or not...'

CHAPTER SEVEN

'I DON'T have to listen to anything you have to say!' Sophie told him quickly.

'No, you don't,' Rafe agreed. 'But you will. Because you won't have a choice.' With that he turned around, locked the bedroom door and pocketed the key while Sophie watched in disbelieving silence.

'You can't do that!'

'Just did.' He strolled across to the window and peered out for a few seconds, his eyes registering the attractive, picture-postcard scenery while his mind sifted through what he was going to say. He turned to face her, propping himself up on the ledge of the bay window, folding his arms. She had, he noticed, managed to scuttle across to the door, not that it would do her much good considering she couldn't open it. Nothing like an old house for a good, old-fashioned sturdy door with lock and key.

'I want you to tell me why you find every way to blacken my character.'

'That's not true!'

'Isn't it? I'm a workaholic with a pathological contempt for the opposite sex. I use them and then I discard them before moving on to yet another notch on the bedpost.'

Sophie stuck her chin up and looked him squarely in the face. 'I can only go on what I see.'

'Which is…?'

'Angela. One minute she's a fixture in your life and the next minute she's disappeared out of the little black book.'

'And that makes me a…?'

'Very unreliable lover.' The word *lover* dropped into the silence between them, strangely hot and intimate and provocative. Belatedly, she realised that she should have chose a more innocuous word, maybe *person*, because now her head was full of images of Rafe and Angela together, rolling around on his king-sized bed, bodies glistening with sweat. She felt sick, like a rag doll propped up against the door.

'And what about my point of view?' Rafe demanded cuttingly. 'Or do your personal prejudices forbid me from having a point of view?'

'I don't have personal prejudices…' Sophie said faintly.

'Oh, we'll come to those later. For the moment, let's talk about my point of view, shall we?'

She knew that she should have been appalled at his accusation of partiality. It was the very worst thing he could level about her considering she was supposed to be doing a piece about him, but for the moment she was too busy contemplating his promise to resume the topic of those personal prejudices. Rather, his threat. It raised the frightening possibility of him chipping away at her defences to expose…*what*? That she was violently attracted to him? Or worse? That she was falling in love with him?

She drew her breath in sharply and watched him the way a mouse watched a cat sharpening its claws a few feet away, getting ready to make its move.

'You seem to think that I use women as playthings…'

'And you don't?'

'Because I don't go out with a woman for the sole purpose of sizing her up as a future life mate, that doesn't mean that I use them as playthings.' Rafe was finding it hard to hang onto his patience. 'Look, my relationships might not lead to the aisle, but I enjoy them and, more importantly, so do the women.'

'It's not that enjoyable when you think a relationship's going to go somewhere and it doesn't.'

'Aren't you viewing that from *your* point of view?' Rafe asked bluntly. 'You happen to think that a relationship is meaningless unless there's marriage at the end of it, and you're assuming the rest of the female population is in agreement with you. Believe it or not, there are a great many women who just want to have a good time, and I show them a good time. They enjoy me as much as I enjoy them and we both recognise that the enjoyment is temporary.' As far as he was concerned, his arguments were perfectly reasonable, so why was he making such a bungled effort at explaining that? He shook his head impatiently and narrowed his eyes. 'Don't tell me that each and every boyfriend you've ever had has been viewed as a possible husband?'

'Of course not!' Each and every boyfriend? Sophie could count on the fingers of one hand how many boyfriends she had had, and she had never gone out with any of them on the mutual understanding that it was all about the physical.

'I don't believe you.' The air between them thickened.

'Actually, I don't care what you believe,' Sophie threw back at him and he smiled, raising his eyebrows with such arrogant disbelief that she wanted to hit him. Particularly as he was right. She did care. A lot. Why else would she have been so inordinately hurt by his past assumptions that she was dull? Inexperienced? A suitable candidate to be looked after? She could feel herself perspiring and knew that if that damned door hadn't been locked she would have taken flight.

'Don't you?' He walked very slowly towards her, enjoying the fact that she had nowhere to run. 'If you're so indifferent to me, how is it that every time I get too close to you you act like a rabbit caught in the glare of approaching headlights, and run for it?'

'Get too close?'

'Metaphorically speaking,' Rafe modified. 'Ask too many personal questions. Raise too many uncomfortable subjects.' He was standing right in front of her now and relishing the delicate bloom of colour that had spread across her cheekbones. He could feel the silent, throbbing charge between them and, from the raggedness of her breathing and the panicked expression in her eyes, he knew that she could feel it too. She might not admit it, but awareness was written all over her.

He felt a peculiar excitement stir inside him.

'I don't answer questions...that is, I try and avoid personal topics because...because...' Her nostrils flared as she breathed him in, that sharp, clean, male scent, undisguised by any synthetic colognes or aftershave. It was like breathing in powerful, mind-altering incense. It made her feel dizzy, did something to her brain so that her thoughts couldn't seem to connect with her vocal cords.

'Because I confuse you?'

'No!' Thank God her vocal cords at least managed that denial!

'Shame.' Rafe shook his head ruefully but his eyes didn't leave her face. 'Because I'd quite like to think that I confuse you...'

Sophie drew in one shaky breath and held it for a few seconds, giving herself time to recover from the effect those casually spoken words were having on her, not to mention his proximity.

'I've avoided personal...conversations with you because...' *because every time you get personal, I walk a couple of metres further along the path of getting emotionally involved with you...because you make my heart race*

'…because it's not my job to share my personal life with you. It's all about *you*, finding out about you, about what makes you tick…'

'Shall I tell you what makes me tick?' He leant into her, palms flat on the door, a living, breathing, potently sexual cage from which she had no chance of escape. 'Curiosity. It's what makes every top businessman tick. Curiosity to push the limits, to find benchmarks that are further and further away, to break new ground…'

Sophie tried hard to focus on the normality of what he was saying, but was ambushed by the roller-coaster rush of her emotions. If only he was would step away, move back to the opposite side of the room, then she would be able to get a grip on herself. With him planted like an immovable object inches away from her, just breathing was an effort, never mind controlling her wildly spinning emotions.

'Are *you* curious?' he asked.

'O-of course I'm curious,' Sophie stammered. 'Aren't we all? Isn't that part of human nature?'

'What are you curious about?'

'What do you mean?'

'What fires up your curiosity?'

'We're supposed to be talking about you.' Sophie tried to drag the conversation back to the prosaic. 'That's my job—'

'Hang the job. The door's locked and I want to know about you. So answer me. What makes Sophie Frey curious?'

'Oh, the usual things.' Her voice sounded faint. A very good representation of how she was feeling, she thought. 'I'd like to travel, see the world, experience different cultures, that sort of thing.'

'What noble intentions,' Rafe murmured. 'A sensible answer.'

'Because I'm a sensible person.'

'Which leads me to wonder whether you've never been curious about what it would be like to shed that sensible self of yours…let yourself go without any thought for the consequences…'

'Why would I do that?'

'Because it might be fun?' He was shrewd enough to appreciate the astounding irony of what he was saying. Doing anything without thought of the consequences was not something he had ever tried. He made money, bought and sold companies, ruled his empire and bedded his woman with one eye always on the consequences, always maintaining control. The tantalising prospect of having this woman in front of him, of not knowing where it would lead because she was an unknown quantity, made every part of him stir with dark excitement. His eyes dropped downwards, leaving her softly parted lips and straying towards her breasts, which were moving in rhythm with her rapid breathing. He knew what those breasts looked like. He just didn't know how they felt, how they tasted.

The thought almost made him groan.

'Fun comes at a price,' Sophie whispered and he nodded, understanding exactly what she was saying, not that he was about to let that dissuade him.

'And sometimes the price is worth paying, wouldn't you agree?'

It was a question to which she was not afforded the opportunity of answering because he dipped his head and then his mouth was covering hers, warm, vital, persuasive.

The battle between common sense and sheer madness lasted a matter of seconds, and then she gave up, handed herself over completely to the dangerous, wonderful immediacy of sensation, pure sensation that stripped her of everything but a powerful yearning that came from deep inside her and spread outwards, devouring everything in its path. She was in love with this man and why shouldn't she have her little window of pleasure? Her heart and her conscience were as one and she returned his kiss, reaching up to link her fingers behind his neck, then through his hair, delighting in the feel of it.

When he lifted her off her feet to carry her to the bed, there was no word of protest. And no word of maidenly shock when he stood back so that he could remove his clothing until he was standing in front of her, one hundred per cent naked, aroused male.

Her eyes feasted on him. It was purely, unashamedly sexual and Rafe had never felt his body respond so dramatically before. He walked towards the side of the bed, watching her watching him, and took her hand in his, guiding it to his magnificent erection, flinging his head back with a groan as she touched it, shyly at first, then with growing confidence.

It took every ounce of will-power not to prematurely end the proceedings when her mouth took over from her hand, licking, exploring, savouring.

He had challenged her to try jumping on the train, destination unknown, to throw caution to the winds and try excitement out for size. He felt as though *he* were the one jumping on the train now. He curled his fingers into her hair and sucked in his breath as he looked down at her, doing such a damn good job of tipping him over the edge.

'No more,' he commanded thickly. Their eyes met, a question in hers, a question laced with amusement. He smiled slowly at her, acknowledging that, right at that very moment, they both knew who was at the controls. 'I'm too close,' he murmured.

Her eyes were filled with smoky promise, which was almost as much of a turn-on as her mouth had been.

'You little minx,' he growled and, with one swift movement, he was over her, straddling her, helping her frantically tug the tee shirt over her head.

His eyes flared in hungry appreciation of what he saw. Those perfect breasts, nipples standing to attention, just begging to be licked. But first he stripped her of the rest of her clothes, tossing the trousers to join his heap on the floor, followed by her underwear. Even with the weak winter sun breaking through the partially drawn-back curtains, her body was flawless. Pale, ivory smooth, the fine hair between her legs proving that she was a genuine redhead.

When he bent to lick one of those rosy peaks, he felt like someone kneeling to pay homage to a goddess. There was no way he was going to rush the experience.

His mission was to taste every inch of her and he was going to do a very thorough job of it. Starting with her breasts, which he kissed, loving the softness of her skin, before indulging in the heady delights of her nipples, suckling on them, drawing them into his mouth until she was squirming under him.

'Not fair!' Sophie gasped. 'You're driving me crazy.'

'Glad it's mutual,' Rafe took time out to reply, their eyes tangling in heated pleasure. He rolled onto his back, pulling her on top of him, then edging her up so that her breasts dangled tantalisingly over his mouth, moving and jiggling and teasing him into the erotic challenge of capturing one of those elusive nipples so that he could continue sucking. As he sucked she gyrated against him, grinding her hips on him.

Gently and expertly, Rafe guided her into a position from which they could confer mutual pleasure on one another, and as she circled his hard erection with her mouth he lost himself in the pleasure of the honeyed sweetness between her legs.

There had never been another woman before her, or at least that was what it felt like as his tongue flicked along the crease, finding the tiny bud that tightened as he licked it. He closed his eyes, just enjoying the taste of her against his mouth, his hands cupping the small, perfect roundness of her buttocks.

He could feel her breasts pushing against him and for an instant he removed his hands from where they were to find those breasts and massage them, rubbing the taut nipples between his fingers, loving the way every touch made her body shudder.

They only broke apart when they both knew, as one, that they had to, that if they continued any longer their love-making would not reach its inevitable conclusion.

And it felt oh, so natural when that inevitable conclusion finally came.

Every pore of her, with every beat of her heart, she was waiting to receive him and it was breathtaking when he entered her, sharply thrusting.

Sophie felt her body nearing its climax and was shocked by the intensity of it when it finally did rip through her, leaving her panting and utterly, blissfully satisfied in its wake.

Rafe seemed to have been affected in the same way. He moved off her and was motionless for a few seconds. He lay on his back, with his eyes closed, and she felt secure enough to look at him without hiding the love in her eyes, only raising her guard when he rolled onto his side and smiled.

'Well, this adds a whole new level to your objective of getting to know the real me...' He gave her a lopsided smile and tucked a stray strand of hair behind her ears, his finger lingering on the lobe, then stroking the sensitive skin just behind it.

'I could tell you what I know I'm supposed to say,' Sophie replied. 'That the journalist should never get involved with her client because work and play never mix…'

'But you're not going to say that, are you?' He laughed off his sudden alarm that she might revert to being the cautious, sensible Sophie with a task at hand.

'How can I?'

'How indeed,' he murmured with satisfaction. 'When I can still taste you on my tongue…' He was gratified to see her blush bright red. 'Besides, strictly speaking, we're more than simply a journalist and a client. We have a history.'

'A history of sorts, anyway.'

'Let's not understate it.' Rafe chuckled. 'Even if we didn't meet regularly, I was still kept informed of your movements by my mother.'

Sophie sighed, understanding what he meant. 'The village grapevine.' He had stopped stroking her ear and was now circling her nipple absent-mindedly with his finger. It felt surreal to be lying in the bed next to him, naked, bodies glistening with perspiration from the aftermath of their passion. Surreal yet at the same time entirely natural.

And that, Sophie thought, was the nature of love. At least for her.

She frowned. 'If they only knew…' She shuddered. Bad enough were they ever to find out that she and Rafe had slept together. Far worse if they ever guessed that, as far as she was concerned, it had been so much more than a carnal act of pleasure.

She looked at him to find his eyes narrowed thoughtfully on her but when she blinked that thoughtful expression was gone, replaced by something more light-hearted.

'You have a fabulous body,' he murmured, a compliment that Sophie refused to consider seriously.

'Bet you tell all the girls that,' she teased, wincing inside.

'I don't, actually.'

'Would that be because they already know?'

'Would that be because I never say something I don't mean?'

'Oh, so none of them had good bodies.' Sophie nodded, considering this option.

'It's not the quality of the body, it's what a woman does with it…'

Sex and flirtation. This was what it was all about, the fun he had spoken about earlier, fun without strings. She had enjoyed it and there was no way she was going to spoil the moment, so she half smiled back at him, nothing serious there.

'Oh. Right.'

'Who taught you?' Rafe kept his voice light and bantering, but there was nothing light inside him when he thought of her in bed with another man.

'Taught me?' Sophie asked in surprise. Then it hit her. She had made love with abandon, with confidence, and no one had taught her that. It was just that this man lying right next to her had brought out the best in her. 'No one taught me,' she admitted, reddening. 'I mean…I'm not the most experienced person on the face of the earth…'

'Define.'

'You want me to tell you how many lovers I've had?' Sophie laughed in mild astonishment, but when he nodded there was nothing amused in his expression.

'Well…one, if you really want to know.' Hell, there was nothing to be ashamed of in that.

'Who was he?'

'Oh, just somebody.' She shrugged airily, edging a bit closer to him because what he was doing to her nipple was getting her heated up all over again.

'Just somebody? I don't believe you.'

'Why not?'

'Because you don't make love with just anybody for the hell of it. He must have meant something to you.'

'Oh, he did.' Sophie thought of Matthew, lovely, caring Matthew who had asked her to be his wife, whom she had very nearly married before she had realised that affection, friendship, pleasant sex, were not necessarily the ingredients for a joyful marriage. Maybe he had belatedly realised that as well, because there had been no weeping and wailing at her refusal, just a calm, measured acceptance for which she had been profoundly grateful. 'We went out for eighteen months and he was the nicest man I have ever known.'

'But nice just didn't do it for you in the end.' *The nicest man she had ever known?* Rafe clenched his teeth together into a sympathetic smile before realising, with satisfaction, that *nice* was the most insulting adjective in the world, especially when applied to a man. Really, it was just *boring* gift-wrapped in shiny paper. 'Did you work with him?'

'No, but I met him through a friend at work. We were friends for quite a while before we became…serious… about one another…' Sophie offered him a slow, sexy smile. 'Why are we talking about this anyway?' She ran one finger lightly down the centre of his chest and he caught it in his hand.

'I thought all women liked to have a conversation after sex.'

Sophie thought that he obviously didn't cater for those women for whom sex with him was a predestined, short-lived occurrence. Yes, she had succumbed to him and, yes, it had been wonderful, better than wonderful, but it would not go beyond this bedroom door. It was her own fault that she had stupidly gone down the falling-in-love route, but no way was she going to compound the error by launching into any kind of affair with him simply because the sex was wonderful. Theirs would be the union of two ships meeting in the night, brushing past one another before drifting out of each other's orbit because that was just the way it had to be.

'Why talk when we can make love?' She gave him a sulky pout, glancing at his sexy face from under her eyelashes, and he grinned at her.

'You do that well.'

'What?'

'That pout thing.' But he still didn't release her hand, even though he was already hardening, wanting to touch her again. 'What's the rush, anyway?' he asked softly.

'The golden oldies might come back any minute…'

'And if they do?'

'Not good.' Sophie shook her head gravely. 'Uh-uh, not good at all.' She reached down and stroked him, felt him move against her fingers. She was a kid with a new toy, but this toy she wanted to keep to herself for ever and, if that wasn't going to be possible, then she wanted to play with it, build up her bank of memories of what it was like, so that she could take the recollection with her for the rest of her life. She wriggled her fingers loose and then guided his hand to where she was already wetly waiting for him, sighing when he cupped her there and began moving his palm against her straining, sensitive womanhood.

'You're right,' Rafe murmured softly, exploring her now with his fingers. 'Best to keep this to ourselves…'

Sophie stilled and Rafe immediately picked up the subtle alteration in the atmosphere.

'There's nothing *to* keep to ourselves,' she said in a quiet voice. She stroked his face, drinking in its angles and contours. 'You were right about taking a chance and having fun just for the sake of it, but only for this one day, Rafe, and then…then we both go back to our own worlds… Lord, why on earth are we being so serious?' She closed her eyes and arched forward, kissing him on the mouth, lingering so that she could taste him completely.

For a few seconds, Rafe looked at her, not understanding what he was feeling, needing in some part of him to prolong the conversation, but her mouth was too persuasive. He returned the kiss, hard, pushing her back while his hands roughly explored the smooth lines of her thigh and the satin softness of her stomach. He was drowning in it when he became vaguely aware of noises in the house.

It took Sophie a few seconds longer to pick up the sounds, then she gave a little yelp and wriggled into a sitting position.

'They're back!'

'It's the wind, that's all. You know these old houses. One gust of wind and anything that can rattle will make sure that it does. Loudly.' He fondled her breast with his hand, like someone weighing a delicacy, while rubbing her nipple with his finger, then he inclined down to take it into his mouth so that he could rasp his tongue against the stiff tip.

He felt her sigh as she relaxed back on the bed with her hand gently in his hair.

But there was no way that either of them could have failed to hear the escalation of noise downstairs, followed by Claudia calling out their names. Sudden panic flared through Sophie and she pushed him off and scrambled off the bed towards the pile of discarded clothes on the ground.

'Get up!' she snapped frantically. 'Or are you going to tell me that old houses can shout?'

Rafe slung both legs over the side of the bed and eyed his bundle of clothes, but before he could make a move towards them Sophie had gathered them up and flung them in his direction.

'Hurry and get dressed! Oh, good Lord...' This last uttered on a groan as footsteps drew closer and there was a loud knock on the door.

'Are you in there, Sophie? The front door wasn't locked...'

'Just coming, Claudia!' Sophie sang out, while she tried to glare Rafe into speedier action. He had managed to pull on his trousers and was now rustling around, feeling in his pockets.

'The key!' she whispered, holding out her hand. 'And make it fast, Rafe. Then you'd better hide...somewhere... in the wardrobe!'

'No way could I fit in that thing.' He was frowning.

'Then *contort* yourself!'

'Are you all right?' Now Claudia sounded concerned.

'Oh, absolutely!' She turned to Rafe. *'The key.'*

'I'm looking, but I can't seem to put my finger on it.'

Sophie's mouth dropped open and she stared at him in horror while he shrugged his shoulders in an infuriatingly Gallic fashion. He seemed to have forgotten about the shirt bit of his ensemble and was strolling towards her, still rooting around in his pockets.

Good Heavens, she thought, how long can it take one very clever man to find a key in a pocket the size of a sock?

'Look harder!' she ordered in a choking undertone. With a sigh of pure exasperation, she raced over to where the clothes had been carelessly tossed and dropped to all fours, face to the floor as she scanned the ground for the delinquent key.

'Found it!'

She spun round, managing just to catch the grin on his

face as he turned towards the door, stuck the key in and opened it. Wide.

Sophie leapt to her feet, bright red as Claudia peeped around her son and received an eyeful of dishevelled, flustered face and clothes that had been thrown on at the speed of light with no time for getting the details right. The button on her trousers was still undone, and Sophie hurriedly clasped her hands in front of her to conceal the incriminating fact.

'Claudia!' she managed weakly. 'You're back early.'

'Too early, from the looks of things.' Finely arched eyebrows raised in an expression of worldly-wise comprehension.

'It's not what you think…' Sophie crossed her fingers in her head for the small but absolutely necessary white lie. 'Rafe was just…on his way out…actually, he just came to give me a few corrections to my report…' She glanced at Rafe for confirmation, which seemed utterly ludicrous considering the man hadn't had the wit to at least get fully clothed. No shirt, and, as her eyes drifted downwards, no shoes either. Unless Claudia had lost her marbles in the space of a couple of hours, she couldn't help but be wondering what the likelihood was of her son coming up to the bedroom to discuss business without a shirt. Or shoes. In winter.

'There's no need to spare my maidenly blushes, Sophie.' Claudia smiled and—good Lord!—winked. Coming from a woman who was so magnificently aristocratic, the wink was almost…almost *indecent*.

'I…' Sophie cast one desperate glance at Rafe, who seemed in no particular rush to help her out of the hole that he had managed to dig by opening the door to his mother.

'I'll leave you two to perhaps join us downstairs? We had planned to have a spot of lunch in town but Maggie's arthritis has been acting up and it seemed a much better idea to just buy one or two things at the shops and come back here to eat. Not that I expect you young things want to hear about the state of our health!'

Sophie smiled weakly and all but groaned.

'It might be an idea, darling, if you stick a shirt on when you decide to join us.' Claudia smiled. Sophie sincerely hoped that another wink wasn't in the offing.

'This is all your fault!' she snapped as soon as Claudia had disappeared, with heaven only knew what tales of unbridled romance and passion to share with Grace. 'Why couldn't you have done what I said? Why couldn't you have just handed me the key and then made yourself scarce?'

'In the wardrobe?'

'In the wardrobe! Behind the bed! Anywhere, Rafe!' She picked up his shirt and flung it straight at him.

'Why are you so worked up about this?'

'Why am I so worked up? Why am I so worked up? Why do you think?' Sophie folded her arms and shot him a look that conveyed the message, *Isn't it glaringly obvious?* 'We had fun but, I told you, it was just a…a…'

'One-night stand?' Rafe offered helpfully.

Sophie blushed, but stood her ground. 'You can call it that if you like.'

'Maybe a one-day stand,' he amended. 'Considering it's still daytime, and there was no way that it had a hope-in-hell chance of progressing into the night.'

'That's right,' she snapped. 'Especially considering Grace and Claudia are in the same house! I don't know how you could have been so…so…*dense*! I told you that I had picked up vibes last night and now here we are. Your mother probably thinks that we're some kind of item and right about now my mother probably thinks the same. I mean, didn't it occur to you at all that answering the door in nothing but a pair of trousers might not have been such a good idea? Answering a locked door?'

'Automatic reaction, I suppose. One key, one door, hey presto.' He savoured the novel sensation of being confronted by a woman agonising over the fact that he was her lover.

'What are we going to do?' she asked bluntly. 'You got us into this mess; you can get us out of it.'

'*I* didn't get us into this mess, Sophie. Our love-making was a mutual decision. The fact is that we're in this situation is because we made love. If we hadn't, the touring party would have returned to find me working and you out, enjoying a walk on the beach. Correct me if I'm wrong.'

Sophie neither agreed nor disagreed. She just stood there looking like a thoroughly maddened little angel. With her trouser button undone.

'Whatever. What do we do now?'

Rafe rubbed his chin thoughtfully and looked at her for a few long seconds in silence before releasing a long sigh.

'We don't have much choice, do we? We'll just have to go with the flow. At least for the remainder of this weekend, my sweet, we have a relationship...'

CHAPTER EIGHT

THE day, which had earlier seemed just a brief blink of an eye during which Sophie could snatch her stolen moment with Rafe, now seemed to stretch out over an endless horizon.

As there was no rush to get downstairs, considering they had supposedly embarked on an exciting, romantic relationship, Sophie took her time having a bath. She assumed Rafe was doing the same. Perhaps if they both showed up freshly laundered, Claudia might think that she had imagined the whole thing.

Lying in the soapy warm water, Sophie tried this idea out for size and reluctantly decided to rule it out.

Which left her glumly contemplating Rafe's plan. A game of make believe.

'You haven't been handed a life sentence,' he had told her impatiently. 'We go along with it and at a later date we can just tell them that we mutually decided to break up. Relationships do that, in case you haven't noticed. It's either that or we say that we were just having a bit of fun.'

Sophie had shuddered at the prospect of that little truth emerging. Her mother, the most generous-minded of people, would have been bitterly disappointed to think that her daughter had taken her clothes off, had had sex simply for the hell of it, because they happened to be under the same roof and human nature had got the better of her. She couldn't bear to think of disappointing her mother. And Claudia would have mirrored those sentiments. A double disappointment. And, naturally, they would see Rafe's behaviour as him simply being a man, according to one of those distasteful but pervasive notions that men somehow were allowed to follow a different set of rules when it came to members of the opposite sex. A man playing the field was simply in the process of looking for the right woman. A woman thought to be playing the field was loose. Not only was Sophie the opposite of loose, but her mother would be deeply worried that her daughter had somehow jettisoned all her principles. And Sophie would have been unable to tell her the truth because that would have been admitting the pathetic fact that she had fallen in love with him.

She dabbed herself dry and chose the drabbest of her outfits to face the waiting crowd. Jeans and a grey loose-fitting shirt that had once been her father's and for which she had a very special affection.

She cuffed the sleeves, slipped on her loafers and pointedly avoided looking in the mirror just in case her eyes showed her too much of what she was really feeling.

Rafe had made it down before her.

She could hear his low, deep, sexy drawl coming from the direction of the kitchen. The drawl got clearer the closer she got.

'It's early days yet, Mother, so there's no point nagging me,' he was saying with a certain amount of smug contentment in his voice. The man was apparently an actor as well as a business tycoon. Maybe the two went hand in hand. Sophie gritted her teeth, took a deep breath and walked into the kitchen where the four women were sitting at the table, sipping cups of tea while Rafe held court standing with his back to her, leaning indolently against the central island.

'I couldn't agree more!' Sophie interjected, making straight for the teapot and pouring herself a cup of tea, even though at nearly midday coffee would have been more to her taste.

'From acorns...' Edith chipped in. 'I never thought Tom and I would end up married and look at us now! I always thought of him as the boy next door, more like a brother than a friend, until one night we went out, just the two of us, because our little party had cancelled out, and we got to chatting. I mean, really talking, and it was like a new world opening up!'

Sophie tried not to choke on her tea at the thought of ever seeing Rafe as *the boy next door* or *like a brother*.

'Yes, sometimes things do work out that way,' Rafe agreed smoothly. He went over to where Sophie was standing, glued to her cup of tea and the square metre of space that was furthest away from him. He slung his arm casually around her neck and toyed with her hair. She tried to smile and look as natural as she could while her mind rapidly flew ahead to that point when they would both diplomatically call the game off and depart their separate ways.

'But more often than not, they don't,' she pointed out, bringing the conversation back down to planet Earth. 'I mean, people have relationships and they just don't last! Especially in London.'

'Why especially in London?' Rafe asked with interest. He managed to sound indulgent and annoyingly sexy when he said that.

'Things are different in London.' Sophie tried to ignore the way he was curling and uncurling strands of her hair around his finger. She stared at her mother, determined to point her in the right direction for disappointment when the phoney love match failed to work out. 'It's not like a cosy little village. It's big, it's fast and everyone moves at a different pace, including their relationships.'

Grace frowned. 'Surely not *everyone*, darling. Or else no one in London would ever settle down, get married...'

'Few do,' Sophie hazarded.

'Unless it's the genuine article.' Rafe gave her a little squeeze of affection and she could have kicked him.

'I quite agree,' Claudia was saying, bustling over to the bags on the counter and pulling out a gourmet assortment of food, which seemed roughly enough to feed double the number of people in the kitchen. 'You mustn't become disillusioned simply because you're in London, Sophie,' she lectured.

Grace added, 'Aand you mustn't think that because the people around you are flitting in and out of relationships that you should do the same. Mind you...' she smiled '...you've never been one to fall victim to peer pressure.'

Which thankfully diverted the conversation onto the general topic of peer pressure, leaving Sophie some time to breathe and also try to wriggle away from Rafe. Her tiny but determined efforts met with no success. He simply tightened his grip on her until she was forced to deliver a substantial prod to his ribs. It did the trick and she escaped fast, before he could recover from the temporary winding.

'No need to give me a hand, Sophie. I've been terribly lazy and bought food that needs absolutely no preparation whatsoever. Just some cold cuts and salad. Not exactly winter warmers, but some hot bread should do the trick.'

'Well, we have the casserole for this evening, Claudia.' This from Maggie who now proceeded to make Sophie's efforts at dodging Rafe utterly redundant by busying herself with setting the table. 'What about you two? Joining us for some lunch, or would you rather do your own thing?' A coy look accompanied this question and Sophie groaned inwardly.

Who would have thought that these women, after decades of experience, were still so stuffed full of romantic notions? So far, not one had taken her up on her tentative remarks about the woeful impermanence of relationships between men and women. She could have been addressing a roomful of sixteen-year-olds! And Rafe had been no help. Instead of helping her cool things down, he had added fuel to their collective fire!

'Oh, I think we'll brave the cold and head for the town,' Rafe drawled, while she was still in the process of working out the pros and cons of staying put as opposed to going out.

'Thought you might!' Claudia laughed and exchanged a glance with Grace. 'You'd better wrap up warm, though, Sophie. It's cold out there.'

'What about all the food?' Sophie asked weakly. 'There's an awful lot... I wouldn't want you to think that you'd wasted your money buying food for us, only for us to disappear...'

'Hungry as a horse, my dear,' Maggie said, and in the ensuing banter Sophie managed to make her exit, with Rafe hard on her heels.

'Spit it out now or wait till we're alone?' he murmured, catching up with her on the stairs and turning her around so that she had to look at him.

'You could have helped me out back there, Rafe!'

'Ah. Thought so. Okay, we'll discuss it over lunch. Meet you by the front door in fifteen minutes.' He sauntered off like a man without a care in the world, leaving her to stew in her own frustration.

Fifteen minutes later, she was ready by the front door, having stuck her head in the kitchen to say goodbye, and her stewing had reached boiling point.

'You're ready to explode, aren't you?' was the first thing

he said, once they were in his car and heading towards the town.

'Ten out of ten for observation, Rafe!' She swivelled to look at his profile, struck against her will by his masculine beauty, two words that had no right to go hand in hand.

'Why? I thought we had agreed that the best option would be to let Grace and Claudia indulge in their little fantasy until we inform them otherwise.'

'I'm glad you used that little word *fantasy*.' The fantasy of being involved with Rafe in a committed and lasting relationship, one involving rings and wedding bells, the fantasy of little Rafe and Sophie children running around in a big garden somewhere, the fantasy of sharing every night with him curled around her in a big bed in a perfect house. It was a cruel joke. 'There was just no need to feed it.'

'You're saying that I should have ignored you in the kitchen? Behaved like an inconsiderate bastard who sleeps with a woman and then treats her like a stranger?'

Sophie didn't say anything. She just stared out of the window and wondered how an unfortunate correlation of random circumstances had contrived to land her up in the place she now was in. Her mind buzzed with *if only* scenarios. If only she hadn't changed jobs; if only she had gone to work for a failing publication; if only Claudia and her mother hadn't stepped in to help her out with her first assignment; if only she had kept herself focused solely on her job and not been distracted by the private man behind the public face. If only she hadn't slept with him.

'I won't do that, Sophie,' he grated coldly. 'I have no intention of projecting a persona that isn't me because it happens to suit you.'

'The more convincing your performance is, the worse it's going to be when the whole thing is called off.' She rested her head against the window and looked at him. 'You've seen for yourself what they're like. Heads stuffed full of cotton candy.'

'Are you telling me that you're a hard-nosed cynic? Because if you are, then I refuse to believe it.'

Sophie wondered whether he liked the thought of her being naïve and gullible. Maybe it gave his ego a boost to think that he was the sexy Svengali showing her the ways of the big, bad world. Hadn't he commented that she needed looking after? Perhaps it gave him a kick to visualise himself in that role. Might make a change from the worldly-wise, sophisticated women he had always dated. Little, lost girl Sophie, fresh out of the country and in need of a masterful man.

'I'm telling you that I'm realistic. Sure, I have the same hopes and dreams about love and happiness as the next person, but I also know that what you and I might have shared, has nothing to do with any of that. And I don't want my mother to be under the illusion that anything is going to come out of it.' She watched as he concentrated on finding a spot to park his car, leaving her remark dangling in the silence.

He only replied when he had manoeuvred into a space. Then he turned to her, his arm resting lightly on the gear lever between them. One hundred per cent undivided attention. She would have to put that in her piece because that was what he did so well. He focused. She had watched him in action, had seen firsthand that peculiar ability he had to mesmerise. It was almost as if he had the ability to will people into listening to what he had to say and into agreeing with him.

Which was why she didn't make the mistake of actually turning to look him in the eye.

'I wasn't pretending earlier, Sophie. I wanted to carry on

touching you.' She heard the half-smile in his voice. 'Not in quite the same way, I grant you, but out-and-out passion is a little tricky in front of parents, wouldn't you agree?'

She wasn't looking at him, but her body was still managing to respond. This was how he did it. He would use that sexy, persuasive voice of his to tell her that there was nothing wrong in touching, in exploring each other, after all they both enjoyed it…wasn't life too short not to enjoy the sensual experiences that were offered? Too short for self-denial? And, of course, she would listen, would see his point of view and would temporarily forget the fact that she wasn't one of those enviable live-for-the-moment types, that in fact she was a boring, down-to-earth type who planned ahead.

'I think we should talk about this over lunch,' was all she said, still staring straight ahead at the picturesque street with its charming shop fronts that managed to be authentically rustic and chic at the same time.

'Okay,' Rafe said, giving in easily. God, he wanted her to look at him, wanted to see what she was thinking, but she wasn't giving an inch. Which was leaving him feeling very frustrated indeed. It occurred to him that he really didn't need to pursue a woman who didn't want to be pursued, but something was dragging him on. He turned away, opened the car door and noticed that she was out of the door before he had time to open it for her. Out of the door and heading up the street with her hands shoved into her coat pockets and a look of frowning concentration on her face.

'I don't know anywhere around here to eat,' she said, pausing as he caught up with her. 'Shall we just make do with a pub lunch or something?'

'Anywhere that involves a table separating us,' Rafe

agreed. 'That way you might be inclined to actually look at me when I'm talking to you.'

Sophie blushed, but didn't rise to the bait. There was a pub to her right. She headed into it, not caring whether it was good or bad. It was good. In fact, it was indistinguishable from the smart, classy pubs that fringed some of London's well-heeled suburbs. The floor was polished wood and the tables and chairs were expensive and plentiful, catering for a clientele that primarily came to eat as opposed to drink.

It was also well on the way to becoming full. They were shown to a table by the window and were handed menus that tried to pass themselves off as café-style, although the list of dishes gave the game away.

'Fascinating menu, don't you agree?'

She looked at him to find him staring back at her with an expression of amusement. He had discarded his menu and was leaning on the table, softly drumming the surface with his fingers.

'It's a shame that these types of places have taken over from the ordinary country pub.' Sophie looked around her at the smart, understated sophistication. 'Not a single Cornish pasty on the menu.'

'Do you like Cornish pasties?'

'Not really, no.' She sighed and dropped the menu. 'Look, I don't want to argue with you, Rafe. I just can't behave like your mistress in front of my mother, especially when I had already reached the conclusion that what we did was…well, wasn't going to be repeated. And don't tell me about Victorian principles and life in the twenty-first century. I know all that. I know that everything you say makes sense to you, but—'

'My mother asked us to stay on with them for a couple more days and I agreed,' he told her bluntly.

Sophie's mouth dropped open. 'You did *what*? When? When did she ask you this?'

'Before you came back downstairs from your bath. I made the mistake of venturing into the kitchen to find out if there was anything I could buy in town, considering their shopping trip had been aborted, and she mentioned it then.'

'And you agreed.'

'It seemed a good idea. For one thing I haven't had a break from work for longer than I want to remember.'

'But that means...'

Rafe gave her a long, assessing look. 'No, it doesn't. I'm more than happy to tell them that it was a one-night affair, that we're far better suited as friends, that sex just clouds the waters. There are a million ways of extricating ourselves from the situation without you feeling that your reputation is being torn to shreds in the process.' He shrugged. 'Give them all the benefit of the doubt. However much they enjoy the thought of the two of us getting together in some desperately romantic clinch, they're old enough to realise that life just doesn't work along those lines.'

'That's not what they were saying earlier on.' Someone came to take their order and Sophie simply followed what he was having because she couldn't be bothered to consult the menu and because her appetite had disappeared anyway.

'You can leave it to me to deal with,' Rafe told her, signalling the waiter over and ordering them both a glass of wine, as well as a bottle of water. 'My sensitivity over what other people think of me is virtually nil and my mother knows me well enough anyway to understand that I would only be speaking the truth if I tell her that there was never any chance of a relationship between us, that we would not wish to jeopardise our newly discovered friendship over sex. That, in fact, there is something honourable about relinquishing a sexual relationship in favour of a platonic one.' His mouth curved into sardonic smile. 'As I am sure that you, too, would agree…?'

'Definitely.' Sophie smiled, but the smile made her mouth ache. Of course, he was absolutely right. Still. She couldn't prevent the stab of disappointment that he had retreated from pursuit so gracefully and so…*quickly*.

The food came, as did the wine. She partook of the latter and toyed with the food while Rafe smoothly changed the subject and asked her all the things a normal person would ask. Things to do with her work and the people she worked with. Boring things. When all she wanted… No, stop right there, she told herself.

'If you like I'll tell my mother that you would prefer us to head back to London. I can always wrap it up in something to do with work. There's always a report that needs urgent attention.'

Sophie looked at him curiously. 'Which makes me wonder what will happen to *your* reports if you decide to take a couple of days off work.'

She allowed him to slip her coat on for her and steeled herself against the soft brush of his fingers against her arm. It was already getting dark outside. The sun had set and a greyish light had settled over everything.

'Sometimes it's wiser not to think along those lines.' He sighed and Sophie flicked him a glance from under her lashes. She hadn't noticed before, but he looked tired and, for the first time, she was ashamed to admit, she realised that he was just human after all. He might have the stamina and energy of something that got plugged into a socket every night, but he was just as prone to exhaustion as the rest of the human race.

'You run your empire, you own every part of it. You

should be able to take however much time off that you feel
you need. I mean, it's not like we ordinary mortals who
have to juggle with calendars and book our time away.'

'Not like you ordinary mortals?' Rafe smiled and
glanced across at her. 'Is that what you think of me? That
I'm not an ordinary mortal?' His low, amused voice did
something funny to her, as did the semi-darkness in the car,
which made it impossible to read any expression on his
face.

'O-of course not...' Sophie stammered. Hadn't she had
firsthand, wonderful experience of exactly how much of a
flesh and blood man he was? Hadn't she touched that beau-
tifully mortal body, every inch of it? She breathed in slowly
and deeply. 'I just mean that you don't have to account to
anybody for your time...'

'Only to myself,' Rafe pointed out, 'and I'm the hardest
taskmaster of the lot.'

'Why would you choose Cornwall for a rest?' she asked,
after a while. 'In winter?'

'The opportunity arose. It seemed like a good idea at the
time. Besides, I like this part of the world and I particularly
like it in winter when the tourists aren't roaming around
every nook and cranny and when the weather can be wild
and unpredictable. It's a very good antidote for a jaded
soul. Now how about that for a confession?'

'There's no need for you to...come back up to London
with me,' Sophie said tentatively. She didn't like the
thought of depriving him of whatever time out he had managed for himself. The situation made her uncomfortable and
so her solution was to escape it. It probably made him
uncomfortable as well, whatever he said about still wanting
her, and yet he had been prepared to see it through for his
mother's sake and because he needed a break. Lord knew,
he probably never had a break if he sat down and thought

about it, but, as he said, the opportunity had presented itself.

'No. I really should get back anyway.' He paused. 'Remember Bob? One of those clients we visited. You laid into me like a bull terrier at the time because I wanted to buy his company which was sitting on some useful land…?'

'Of course I remember him. His company made furniture.'

'He agreed to the deal.'

'To sell to you?'

'Shocking, isn't it? He worked out that going to the wall was a far worse proposition than flogging his company to me at a very generous price. In other words, he saw the light of day.'

'In other words he saw the torchlight you held up and shone in front of him, while you convinced him that what he was seeing was in fact the light of day.'

'I love the way you don't pull your punches.' Rafe laughed and she realised that neither of them had laughed since leaving that bedroom. She had sniped at him, making him pay for her own disaster, and he had stoically maintained a composed front, gritting his teeth in the process. 'We came to an amicable agreement, put it that way.'

'Which would be what?'

'He sold to me and I'm still going to put up my out-of-town shopping centre, but it's going to be more along the lines of a craft centre and Bob will have as much input as he can handle in designing it, along with my team of architects. He was, to put it mildly, happy with the outcome.'

Sophie looked at him in amazement. 'You mean you sacrificed your plans for his sake?'

'I mean we reached an agreement. One that I am personally very pleased with. And that, amongst other things, can usefully be completed if we both return to London in the morning.'

'I suppose it wouldn't hurt if I stayed on for a couple of days…'

'Don't agree to anything you're not comfortable with, but, unless you want us to break the news to the old dears that their match made in heaven isn't quite as it seems, then you're going to have to swallow and put up with the fact that we might have to withstand a few conspiratorial looks, and several more anecdotes about finding true love against all odds.'

Sophie smiled reluctantly. Had she overreacted? It wouldn't be the first time since she had been around him.

'I think I can withstand it. And maybe it will give a more rounded picture of you. At work and at rest, so to speak. See what you do when you're relaxing.'

Approaching it from a work angle immediately made her feel more comfortable with the prospect of two or three more days in his company. She had travelled with her laptop computer and she would have ample time to completely finish her assignment and get him to proofread it. It made sense. Didn't it?

'But I don't think it's a good idea to give them false hope, to act as though we're lovestruck.' She laughed, pleased that she sounded so casual. 'It's not as though we're teenagers any more. No one expects two grown adults to act like adolescents.'

'Up to you.'

'What does that mean?'

'It means that I will be the perfect gentleman.'

'Good.' Did she believe him? Yes, she did. Because, however much he wanted her, he didn't want her enough, not enough to wage a war with his self-control. She wondered whether he was capable of loving any woman enough for that. To truly love someone meant opening yourself up to vulnerabilities, and Rafe would never do that. The hopelessness of the situation in which she found herself hit her like a tidal wave of dull despair.

They arrived back at the house to find a note pinned to the kitchen counter. Energy had been rallied, it seemed, and the four women had decided on a walk along the beach.

'In the dark? And cold?' Sophie wondered aloud, removing her jacket and walking over to the kettle. 'What possessed them?'

'A beach at night can be an extremely calming experience,' Rafe countered.

'Can it? Would you like some coffee?'

'Yes to both questions.' He had moved to the kitchen table and taken up residence there, leaning back against a chair, eyes closed.

'You look exhausted,' Sophie said, turning away and addressing the kettle.

'Do I? It comes with the territory, I suppose.'

'A lot seems to come with this territory of yours, Rafe.'

'For instance?' He couldn't work out when exactly it had happened, but somewhere along the line he had become accustomed to her questions, the ones that breached his private boundaries. He half opened his eyes and watched her as she made them both a cup of coffee. Her movements were calm and measured. Until she came near him, and then it all went pear-shaped. It was an incredible turn-on.

'No rest or relaxation…'

'Perhaps not the rest, but I do have my methods of relaxation.' As he expected, she allowed this ambiguous comment to go unanswered. 'I read,' he expanded lazily. 'Listen to music, occasionally watch television…'

'Oh!' Sophie glanced up at him, then back down at the

coffee, which was in the process of being stirred to death, ashamed of her seedy mind, which had immediately linked *sex* with *relaxation*. 'What do you read?'

'Biographies. Anything written by war reporters. Various newspapers every day. Music, any and everything, but I have a soft spot for jazz. Television—well, that's a bit harder...'

'Because once the news has come to an end, it just really leaves a diet of reality shows, soap operas and reruns?' Sophie deposited his cup in front of him and then removed herself to the opposite end of the table.

'Don't knock those soap operas, although I confess that they do tend to either become exceedingly dreary or else ludicrously unreal in their pursuit of high ratings.'

'You don't really watch soap operas! Do you?'

Rafe gave her one of those speciality crooked smiles that made her pulses go into mad overdrive. 'Off and on. When I happen to be at home in the same room as a television set at the right time. Sometimes it beats the news when it comes to relieving stress. Course, that doesn't happen very often because I'm not actually mortal and am deprived of the ability to do the sort of normal things that ordinary people do.'

'If you had a family to go back to, you might find it easier to wind down. I mean, you might have a reason for not spending so much of your time working...'

'Are you offering that observation in your professional capacity as someone trying to find out what makes me tick, or are you just displaying female curiosity in my single status?' The flip side of his crooked smile was the expression on his face now, mildly attentive, but mostly on the wrong side of bored.

'Does it matter? Wouldn't the answer be the same?' She wondered whether she was capable of asking him anything in a truly professional capacity now. Every question, every remark would be tinged with that intimate knowledge of him and her own recognition of her feelings for him.

For a few seconds, Rafe didn't say anything. Then he leant back into his chair and folded his hands behind his head, tilting back so that he was staring at her broodingly, through half-closed eyes.

'Why is it that women are so damned keen to find out why I haven't got a wife? Or, dreadful term, *a significant other*? I'm sure if I were being interviewed by a man, I would never get asked the question you just asked me.' He gave her a few moments to digest this before continuing softly, 'I enjoy my life the way it is. Maybe you're right. Maybe if I had the little family back at the ranch, I'd be joining the mass office exodus at five-thirty every evening so that I could rush back to the warm, cosy place with the smell of home-cooked food. Unfortunately, if it worked as smoothly as that, there would be no divorce, would there? No, along with the little woman at home comes all sorts of problems. The glorious creature you imagine you want to spend the rest of your days with can quickly turn into a shrew and a harpy and the home-cooked meal…well, it starts off just fine, but how long before the recipe books get replaced by the fast-food containers? I have a very good friend whose life was perfectly uncomplicated for years. He lived in happy partnership with a very beautiful girl, and then they married. Within two years, things had become so unbearable that they found themselves at a marriage-counselling service trying to find out where things had gone wrong.'

'Why would they do that?' Sophie asked with just the right note of wry airiness that she knew would meet with his approval. 'When they could just come to you instead, since you obviously have all the answers?'

Sure enough, he responded with appreciation, his sexy eyes flickering with shared amusement. 'Not *all* the answers,' Rafe mused, wishing that the length of the table didn't separate them, but grateful for it because he didn't want to find himself suddenly out of control, unable to resist touching her, even though he knew that she would probably run a mile. Chasing a woman determined to run in the opposite direction was just not his style, but this woman…

'Just sufficient for me to tell you what you probably already know for yourself. After all, you seem to be the expert on analysing my character. I'm not the marrying sort of man. In fact, the thought of marriage leaves me cold. My mother might be excited at the prospect of a girl she knows and approves of being on the horizon. Maybe you're right, maybe she's already dreaming of wedding bells and planning which hat she'll wear, but…' He shrugged, not feeling the need to finish his sentence because his meaning was as clear as daylight.

Sophie got the message loud and clear. He was warning her off, telling her in so many words that he wasn't up for grabs. He could do lust, he just couldn't do love and he wasn't about to string her along with promises he had no intention of keeping.

There was no need for him to state the obvious! Her coffee was gently coagulating in front of her, but she still took a tiny mouthful, to give herself something to do.

'Which still leaves us where we were at the very beginning, before you got spooked by my mother discovering us…*in situ*, so to speak.'

'Which is where?'

'Two people who want each other.'

Sophie opened her mouth to vigorously deny any such thing and closed it again just as quickly. She could deny until she went blue in the face, but it would be a lie. He knew it and so did she. What he didn't know was how much more she wanted, which was why he was so keen to set his parameters, just so that unfortunate misunderstandings didn't occur. How thoughtful of him.

'What I want is for you to do as you promised, behave like a—a gentleman.'

'And what *I* want,' Rafe said with a soft, assessing smile that made her toes curl, 'is for you to stop hiding from the inevitable and come to me…'

CHAPTER NINE

RAFE was being the perfect gentleman. Sophie had had a full day of it and had already long gone past the point of wondering why she had ever agreed to stay on for just a few days more. Just being around him was driving her crazy, even though he was no longer using every opportunity of touching her whenever he felt the situation demanded it. Instead, he was deeply considerate and the touching was replaced by *looking*, which was almost as torturously seductive. He would sit at the opposite end of the table, because they had spent the day out with the rest of the party, and he would *look* at her. Oh, he would chat to everyone, he would be charming and witty and informative, but his eyes would be on her the whole time, as though he were somehow having a private conversation only with her, something intensely sexy that was taking place underneath the formal chit-chat that was directed to everyone else.

And now, here she was, at a little before seven in the evening, having to listen to her mother rhapsodise about him.

'The way he looks at you, darling...' Grace was lying on the bed, watching as her daughter applied some make-up, having jollied her into wearing the new outfit she had treated her to earlier on in a shopping trip. Mother and daughter had branched out for a couple of hours, the object of which, as it transpired, was to purchase some clothes for her. Obviously the drabness of her outfit the evening before had jostled her mother into thinking that a new wardrobe was called for, despite Sophie's vehement denials that she needed to dress up for a stay in the cottage.

Now, kitted out in a figure-hugging woollen skirt and an even more figure-hugging short-sleeved top, Sophie met her mother's interested gaze in the mirror.

'He doesn't *look* at me, Mother.'

'Oh, but he does. Scorching looks.'

Sophie all but groaned aloud. 'He's a very physical man. I mean, he's someone who enjoys…well…' She baulked at the thought of spelling it out in black and white. Some things went beyond the call of mother/daughter bonding. Instead, she chose to change the subject. 'I thought you didn't like these kinds of clothes, anyway.' She stood up and made a sweeping gesture at herself. 'I thought,' she continued accusingly, 'you approved of comfortable clothes, because it's what's inside that counts. I feel like a fool.' Which meant that she felt *on show*, when what she wanted was to keep the whole thing low-key, perhaps just slide casually into the *friends only* bracket.

'You look delightful.' Her mother smiled approvingly. 'And besides, what you're wearing is practical. Lovely and warm for winter, but feminine as well. I think, and I might be wrong, that Rafe is the sort of man who likes women to be well dressed.'

'I don't care what Rafe likes!'

'That,' Grace said comfortably, 'is probably because you feel so at ease around him.'

Sophie nearly spluttered in sheer amazement at the ludicrous misinterpretation of what she had said. But there wasn't much she could say as her mother swept on with an involved analysis of the importance of feeling comfortable with one's partner, being able to just be oneself in front of them, to know that they will accept you, warts and all. Sophie was beginning to wonder whether she was the only sane person left in the world, or at least in this small cottage in Cornwall.

'Just between the two of us, Claudia and I were beginning to wonder whether the pair of you would ever settle down.'

Sophie's mouth dropped open. 'You mean you've been gossiping about us behind our backs?'

'I don't much like the word *gossiping*,' Grace said calmly, standing up to rearrange her daughter slightly, then edging backwards to cast a critical but approving eye at the finished product. 'Of course we chatted to one another about both of you. Claudia and I are good friends and we love you both so much.' She stroked her daughter's hair fondly.

'Which is lovely,' Sophie said, determined to keep her head and take a grip on the spiralling situation. 'But, as I said, Rafe and I are not looking for anything permanent. He's not a committing kind of man.' That much, at any rate, was the utter truth. 'He likes playing the field and, for a man like Rafe Loro, there's an awful lot of field to play with.' She hoped the look she gave her mother was a knowing one.

'We'll see,' Grace murmured, which made Sophie want to scream in frustration. Instead she gave a dry laugh.

'Indeed we will!' It was a cynical rejoinder aimed at a disappearing back as Grace headed out of the bedroom. Sophie wasn't even sure her mother had heard.

There was no sign of Rafe downstairs. Nor, when she went to the kitchen, was the table laid out for six.

'We've decided to have a light supper and play some more bridge,' Claudia said, eyeing Sophie and then nodding at Grace.

'I saw that look, Claudia,' Sophie admonished. 'I suppose you two cooked up this whole thing? The shopping trip? The new outfit? You're both as transparent as…as glass!'

'Just two old women having fun,' Claudia replied serenely. 'You wouldn't want to deny us that, would you? Now, shoo! Rafe is waiting for you.'

'Waiting? Waiting where?'

'It's nothing fancy, but we all thought it would be lovely if you two had a romantic meal on your own. After all, you've been trekking around with us all day.'

'A romantic meal?'

'Joint effort,' Maggie said briskly. 'Fish. Quick and easy when you know how. A few vegetables, bought pudding, I fear.'

Sophie was bewildered, until it dawned that a meal had been prepared for her and Rafe.

'Best bit,' Claudia added mischievously, 'is that we've thoroughly spoilt ourselves by getting little Annie over to do the washing-up for us. Oh, and the waitressing! She was absolutely delighted. Apparently Christmas has left her with a nasty debt.' Annie was the girl who came and cleaned the cottage out every other weekend, even when it was not being used. She aired and dusted and made sure that nothing had leaked, burst or otherwise done anything untoward.

'It's just so wonderful having the two of you here,' Claudia said truthfully, 'that it's nice to spoil you a bit.' Everyone was nodding. Sophie felt trapped in a world in which she no longer had any say over what happened to her.

'Rafe's waiting in the sitting room for you,' Claudia continued. 'And I don't want you two to even think of coming into the kitchen! You're to enjoy yourselves.'

'And leave us four to at least *try* and concentrate on the bridge, if we can get past the chat!' This from Edith, who was pouring the wine. Sophie doubted concentration was going to stand much of a chance if the glasses were topped up quite so generously. But she wasn't allowed to waste time debating the point. They were all sending her out and none of them, she concluded, was a mind-reader. Including her mother. If they were, they would have realised that the very last thing she wanted was a romantic meal with Rafe Loro.

Rafe was waiting for her in the sitting room.

'Ah. You're here. It seems we have been manoeuvred.' His eyes flicked over her. She looked…edible, like a feisty, wilful child wrapped up in elegant clothes and the most appealing thing was that she was so unaware of it. Unaware of the impact she made on men. He wanted to kiss the scowl off her face, but he remained just where he was, looking at her. She would come to him.

'Did you know about this?' Sophie demanded.

'Yes. About half an hour ago when my mother came up to my room and revealed that a meal would be laid on for us. Why don't you stop hovering by the door and sit down? I'll get you a drink.' He didn't wait for her answer. Instead, he stood up and strolled over to a table, on which was an ice bucket holding a bottle of wine, and some glasses. Sophie accepted the drink and waited for him to return to his chair.

He looked dazzlingly attractive. The casual look had been jettisoned in favour of dark trousers and a black crew-necked jumper, which made him look rakishly handsome.

'You might as well enjoy it,' he advised, and Sophie frowned suspiciously.

'Enjoy what?' She opted for the sofa, which was close enough to avoid having to shout at him across the width of the room and far enough so that any accidental physical contact was out of the question.

'Tonight.' He shrugged. 'They've put themselves out and, whether you like it or not, it would be churlish not to at least put on an act of appreciation.'

Sophie drank a long mouthful of wine and sighed. 'I hate being manipulated.'

'So do I.' Rafe shrugged and sipped some of his drink, watching her carefully over the rim of his glass as he did so. 'But we can humour them while we're here, at any rate. When we're on our own, you can drop the act and talk about work if you like.'

'It doesn't bother you, does it?' Sophie asked bitterly. 'You don't really care that this whole thing is spiralling out of control, do you? I had my mother with me for the better part of an hour this evening and she's…well, her head is in the clouds!' Sophie drank the remainder of her wine, which, at least, was having the desired effect of bucking up her spirits.

'Then just put up with it until we leave.'

'Easier said than done.'

'No. Actually, it's not.' He stood up and walked over to where she was sitting and proceeded to position himself right next to her. 'Instead of whingeing and moaning, why don't you just relax? You won't change anything by tying yourself in knots. They think that we're an item and it may be a bit uncomfortable for you but, face it, their opinions don't actually commit us to anything. It's not as though we're going to be talked into the nearest register office over the space of two days.'

'Thank you for that,' Sophie said coldly. 'But I'm not as accustomed as you are to ignoring how other people feel and just doing what I want.'

Rafe muttered an oath under his breath and looked at her steadily. 'I am not going to initiate a war of words with you,' he said coolly. 'But what I will tell you is this: we are going to go into that dining room and enjoy the meal that has been kindly and lovingly cooked for us and we are going to converse with each other like two civil adults and you are not going to bristle because of those damned principles that you are chained to!'

Sophie's face drained of colour. He had taken small stabs at her before, but this was the first time he had flatly told her exactly what he thought.

'I am not chained to my principles!' she defended herself angrily, expecting retaliation, but there was none. He just continued to look at her with that steely glint in his eyes before rising to his feet and heading to the door.

'I'm not about to argue with you, Sophie. We'll eat dinner, we'll compliment the chefs and tomorrow we'll leave first thing in the morning.'

Sophie followed him into the dining room. It was small and cosy and decorated in deep reds and burnished golds that lent it a warm, intimate air. And the table was set with the best crockery and candles. A spirited effort for the young lovers, or so Claudia and Grace would have imagined.

She suddenly saw things from Rafe's perspective. He hadn't been out to deceive them, merely to accommodate them until the time came when they could be let down gently.

She, on the other hand, had taken the straightforward approach of being as honest as she could within the confines of the situation and so had ended up being…sounding…at least to Rafe, childish and mutinous.

She looked at his cold face and her heart sank. The light-hearted teasing and the flirting, which she had warned him not to do, because her beloved principles wouldn't allow it and because she was so damned terrified of what it did to her, had gone. The man facing her across the table was the same man she had first set eyes on when she had appeared in his office on an assignment neither of them had wanted. He had, quite simply, got fed up of her and she wondered whether she could blame him.

It was like having a source of warmth suddenly removed, and the removal was not of her doing, and the icy chill left behind hurt her more than she thought possible.

She fiddled with the stem of her empty wineglass. There were two wineglasses, one for white and one for red, and an assortment of cutlery, which made her think that the hurriedly prepared meal must have taken longer than her mother had intimated. While she had been gently encouraged up to her bedroom to rest and relax, they had been scurrying around the kitchen preparing a meal and happily sharpening their matchmaking knives.

She expected that Rafe, too, would have been urged to maybe disappear and relax. She doubted he would have nodded off, which was what she had done. He might have worked. In fact, he probably had, and emerged to discover the same as she had, but, instead of railing against fate, he had calmly accepted it and now…now he was just plain fed up with her, fed up with her incomprehensible behaviour. One minute she was flinging herself at him, the next minute she was backing away as though her life depended on it.

'If I've spoilt your short break, I'm sorry,' Sophie mumbled, not quite meeting his eyes.

'Forget it.' He poured them both some more wine. 'I should have realised that staying on here was a mistake.'

'I'm sorry.'

'What are you apologising for this time?'

Sophie took a deep breath and met his eyes across the table. With just four candles illuminating the room, it was impossible to read any expression on his face, but his voice told its own story. 'I gave you mixed messages. I don't know what you think of me, but…'

'Drop it, Sophie. What I think of you isn't important.'

But it was. Right now it felt as though nothing in the world was as important as what he thought of her. 'Of course it is. I wouldn't want you to think that I'm not a professional.' Or a prissy, screwed-up mess, she added to herself. Someone old enough to know her mind but still incapable of moderating her behaviour. Someone whose veneer of professional competence was constantly being hijacked by her own stupid, immature, emotional inconsistency.

'Don't worry. I won't run to your boss and spill the beans about us having slept together. Rest assured that you'll walk away with your assignment successfully completed and your pride intact.'

Annie came in with their starters, which she nervously set in front of them, accompanied with a monologue about how nice it was to see the cottage being used, and Sophie stared down at the bowl of soup, dismally aware that she had no right to pursue any kind of personal conversation with Rafe and, if she did, even less right to assume that he would respond. Why should he? The soup was freshly made daily and sold in one of the shops in the town, and it smelled delicious, but her appetite seemed to have deserted her.

'Eat it,' Rafe ordered icily. 'You won't be sending any food back untouched.'

'Stop ordering me around!'

'Then start acting like an adult!'

Sophie glared at him, infused with a sudden burst of anger, which was a damned sight easier to handle than the miserable sense of guilt she had been feeling.

'By which you mean listen to what you have to say and do exactly what you want?'

'You can translate it any way you like.'

He, at any rate, seemed to have no problem with his appetite. He was clearly enjoying the soup and bread, if not the company. And he was looking at her as if she were a stranger, someone he had found himself having to share a meal with, and who required effort.

'And you don't give a damn what I think either way. Is that it?'

His silence only infuriated her further. He had picked her up, she hadn't played the game his way and so now he had discarded her. She attacked her soup with one of the rolls and enjoyed her anger. It was so much easier being angry with him than with herself.

'I'll let you know when I read your finished article,' Rafe said noncommittally, shoving his bowl and saucer to one side and leaning back in his chair so that he could give her the full benefit of his hard, remote face. 'Did you enjoy the soup?'

'Fine.'

'Amazing what you can buy from a shop nowadays. Almost makes the culinary arts redundant, wouldn't you agree?'

'I haven't given it much thought.' This was what she had wanted. Nothing personal. Now that she was on the receiving end of it, though, it wasn't nearly as satisfying as she would have expected. She didn't want to see his tight, closed face. She didn't want to converse about nothing in particular.

'No?' His voice was mildly interested. In a minute she expected him to glance at his watch. Nothing too obvious, but just a quick reminder of how much longer he would have to endure her company.

Not, she told herself quickly, that she wanted him trying to get her into bed. Oh, no! He might laugh at her boring principles, but they would save her from being hurt, and that was a very good thing.

'I thought that, being on your own, you would have discovered all the short cuts when it comes to food.'

'I might say the same about you,' Sophie retorted.

'I rarely eat in on my own.'

'No, sorry, I forgot. That would be because you're not chained to any dreary principles!'

'Didn't care for that remark, did you, Sophie? Was it just a little too close to the truth for comfort?'

'Yes, I have principles. I work by my own set of right and wrong codes—'

'And when a little genuine emotion shoves them through the window, you just can't cope with it. And yet you tell me that you're not chained to your principles! A little hypocritical, wouldn't you say? Has it occurred to you that even your mother is pleased to see you having a good time? Maybe more pleased than thinking that you're cooped up in London, spending Saturdays on your own while you wait for Mr Permanent to walk through the door and ask for your hand in marriage!'

Sophie felt colour crawl into her face. She linked her fingers together on her lap and, however much she hated him for the accusations he had just thrown at her, her mind refused to treat them with the contempt they so rightly deserved. Instead, it played with the possibility that he might be right. Was that how her mother felt? That she, Sophie, was holed up somewhere in cloud-cuckoo-land, waiting for her Prince Charming to appear, and until such time was content to sit it out somewhere, gathering cobwebs and eating TV dinners on her own?

'She's only pleased because she thinks that we're going

to get married!' Sophie snapped. 'Which isn't that surprising given the sterling act you've put on for their benefit!'

'Oh, for God's sake.'

There ensued ten minutes of charged silence as Annie entered to take away their bowls and lavish praise on the main course that she was about to bring in.

His accusations of hypocrisy had time enough to ferment in her head.

What was it about him? Why did he make her behave in ways that astonished her? She fought to hold onto the reins of self-control before they deserted her completely, and by the time Annie had placed the fish in front of them she found that she could manage a halfway decent smile. Just so long as she didn't concentrate too hard on the unforgiving angles of his face.

'I think it's wonderful what you did to Bob,' she said neutrally, harking back to a topic of conversation that had come and gone because it was the least incendiary one she could think of. 'I know you would rather that I don't mention anything specific in my article, but would you allow me to use that?'

'If you like.'

Silence. Sophie resisted the urge to bristle. 'This fish is delicious.' She took another stab at innocuous conversation. 'I've always thought that Maggie missed her calling as a chef.' More silence. 'And I suppose you're going to sit through the rest of this meal in silence?' she asked politely. 'A bit childish, wouldn't you say?'

Childish? Rafe nearly choked on his mouthful of food. Apart from anything else, he couldn't remember having ever been labelled childish by anyone. Not even as a child.

Green eyes tangled with blue. 'You,' he said, 'are the most complicated, unpredictable woman I have ever met in my entire life!'

'I'll take that as a compliment,' Sophie returned. 'It's better than dull, boring and prim.'

'I don't recall having used those adjectives to describe you.'

The relief of having him talk to her made her feel giddy. Anything but that flat, cold look and that dismissive tone of voice.

'You implied it,' she said, tucking into the fish with more gusto than she had done with the soup. 'Well, you implied that I was a country bumpkin who needed looking after. How many riveting, scintillating country bumpkins do you know?'

'You're not experienced when it comes to the ways of the world. Adrian would have eaten you up and spat you out for breakfast.'

And you wouldn't? Sophie wanted to know. Yes, of course he would, but there was a big difference. In his case, she would have enjoyed the experience, would have sacrificed the misery of being rejected as a fair trade-off for the joy of being wanted, even for a short space of time. Her desperation to run away from him was fear, and what kind of life would she have if she allowed her head to make every emotional decision for her? An ecstatically happy and exciting life with someone who fulfilled all the right requirements on paper, but never in practice?

'So what?'

'*So what?*' Rafe exploded. He pushed his plate away and Sophie raised her eyebrows wryly.

'I thought we had to finish every scrap of food?'

Rafe ignored her. He folded his arms and if it weren't for the way his teeth were clamped tightly shut, he would have almost passed as being in control.

Was he jealous? she wondered. Just thinking along those lines made her stomach lurch in sharp excitement.

'He *was* rather good-looking...' she said, cupping her chin in her hand and staring off into the distance. 'Dashing.'

'Which just goes to show how green around the gills you are when it comes to judging the opposite sex,' Rafe inserted bluntly. 'Even if his reputation didn't precede him, most women with even a fraction of experience would be able to tell at a glance that Adrian Walsh is a player.'

'And you aren't?' Sophie asked with interest, her eyes sliding over to his face and noting that he had the grace to flush.

'I'm honest in my dealings with women,' he countered without missing a beat. 'And when I'm with them...' his eyes did a long, leisurely appraisal of her '...I give everything, or so I like to think. Tell me if you don't agree...' His smile was as lazy as the expression in his eyes and it brought a wave of hot colour to her face. 'Good Lord, you seem to have been rendered speechless.' The wicked ghost of a smile tugged the corners of his mouth.

'You mean you want me to rate you as...as a...'

'You can say it,' Rafe coaxed softly, watching her. '*Lover.* I know you want to distance yourself from the situation, but you can't make the reality of what happened between us disappear...' He could feel himself hardening, craving the release of making love with her, plunging into that sweet, honeyed wetness that he knew he could arouse. He wondered whether she was feeling it too, feeling herself moisten down there, wanting him... Thank God for the table separating them because his erection was blatantly obvious.

Sophie inhaled deeply and looked him straight in the eye. 'You want me to rate you as a lover? Is that it? That's a little bit conceited, isn't it?'

'Thank you,' Rafe drawled.

'I haven't given you my opinion yet.'

'Oh, but you have. Why else would you think me conceited if I wasn't going to hear what I wanted to hear?'

Sophie was barely aware of Annie coming in and clearing away their second course. She heard background chatter, knew that something was being placed in front of her, presumably the store-bought dessert that Maggie had apologised for earlier on, knew too that coffee and cups were being laid out on the sideboard, but all that was happening in her peripheral vision. She couldn't take her eyes off Rafe's face. Right now, though, she didn't feel like a rabbit trapped in the headlights of a fast-approaching car. Right now, she felt empowered. She wasn't going to run away again, scuttling in panic to find the safest corner to hide behind, from which she could peer at Life without dipping her toes in if she didn't want to. Her fear of disappointment and unhappiness was a damn sight more bearable than the sickening fear she had felt when he had withdrawn from her.

'Okay. You're good. No, better than good. Not, as you point out, that I'm any kind of judge.'

Rafe stuck his spoon into some of the dessert. It was a trifle of sorts. Sophie played with hers. 'Try some,' he said. He heaped some on his spoon and stretched across, with Sophie pausing only fractionally before she leant towards him and lowered her eyes to eat what was being offered.

Okay. So what if she had no idea how women gave men the 'come hither' look? She could try. Tonight she had come crashing into her own desires. They had pushed their way through her self-protection mechanism and there was no way she could ignore them. She wanted him and to hell with common sense and doing the logical thing for her future peace of mind. One way or the other, she knew that she would never have that again. Either she allowed him to walk away thinking the worst of her, thinking that she was tied, gagged and bound by her rigid principles and incapable of shaking them, or else she started enjoying what was in front of her and walked away when she sensed that she was beginning to bore him. How long that would take, she had no idea. A week? A month? Six months? His track record spoke for itself, but she wasn't going to let that deter her. Not now.

She opened her eyes to find him inches away from her, staring straight back.

Both hands were firmly propped on the table, and she could feel herself trembling.

She deliberately took her time licking the spoon, willing him to follow the lead being laid down. He didn't.

She wondered if perhaps her seductive gesture hadn't been quite up to scratch. Had she ended up looking ridiculous?

Worse, and it was hard to imagine a worse scenario, maybe he had been so turned off by her incomprehensible behaviour that it didn't matter whether she licked a spoon slowly or quickly or even stood on the table and did a striptease, he was no longer interested.

The thoughts flashed through her head at the speed of light. She was looking down at herself and seeing him laughing at her, with her gauche, inept imitation of a vamp…seeing him feeling a range of responses from disgust to boredom, with desire not featuring on the menu, because she had blown it.

Her instincts told her to politely resume her seat, say something complimentary about the trifle, ask him a few sensible questions about getting a photographer in to take a few pictures of him for her article, pretend that they were still just two civilised adults who had had a very brief fling and had now put the memory of it behind them.

Or she could just go hell for leather and kiss him.

She reached up and placed her hand behind his neck, and her mind went blank. No more analysing what he might be thinking or feeling and no more wondering whether she was doing the right thing or the wrong thing.

She pulled him towards her and kissed him. His mouth still had the sweet taste of the trifle she had just eaten. She half expected him to pull away, but he didn't, although he might have just been stunned into a lack of immediate response. She couldn't tell because her eyes were now firmly shut against any unfortunate reactions.

Then he was returning that kiss, his mouth moving over hers, hungrily demanding.

Lord only knew where the spoon was. Probably leaving an indelible stain somewhere on the white linen tablecloth, which Sophie was sure had all been part of that special effort laid on by their mothers.

Of course, sooner or later they both had to surface for air, and Sophie hoped that no questions would be asked. No such luck. Still awkwardly inclined across the width of the table, Rafe was the first to draw back and she reluctantly opened her eyes.

'Care to tell me what's going on here?' he asked thickly.

Sophie looked down, then back up at him, squaring her chin.

'I can't fight any more.'

'I didn't realise that we had been fighting.' It occurred to him that this was not a comfortable position in which to be conducting this conversation. He was too tall, and it required a certain amount of dexterity to avoid the array of glasses on the table, but he was loathe to let her go.

'Not with you,' Sophie admitted, bracing herself to reveal the truth, well or a bit of it, at any rate. 'I wasn't talking about fighting with you. I was talking about fighting with myself. It's what I've been doing ever since…ever since…we made love. As relationship material goes,' she continued truthfully, 'you're not the stuff of any girl's dreams. At least not any girl with her head screwed on the right way. But I…I realise that…you know what I want to say…'

'Do I?' Rafe realised that he was thoroughly enjoying himself. 'I'm not sure that I do. Perhaps you could spell it out for me?'

Sophie took a deep breath. Saying what she had to say while maintaining eye-to-eye contact was an almost impossible task, but she did it. She kept her eyes firmly locked with his.

'I want you,' she said in a rush. 'Crazy, but there you have it.'

'I'm not sure I like the *crazy* part…' Rafe allowed a few seconds to tick past. 'But I like the rest of it.' He kissed her gently and very, very thoroughly until she was moaning softly under her breath, her mouth blindly seeking his out when he eventually drew back.

'Maybe we could take our coffee into more…agreeable surroundings,' he suggested, and Sophie found that she was nodding eagerly.

'We should thank…well, everyone, for the lovely meal,' she suggested.

'Oh, I'm sure they would understand if we disappeared without that formality,' Rafe murmured, moving towards the door and waiting for her. The coffee was forgotten on the sideboard, a signal to Annie that they wouldn't want to be disturbed. And if that wasn't enough, well, then, these old houses, as he had discovered, were well endowed with locks.

CHAPTER TEN

SOPHIE stared out of the window of the office. Not much of a view, but the sun was still trying to make the most of things. Behind her, her successful article on RAFE LORO— THE MAN BEHIND THE REPUTATION was framed, a testimony to her first successful assignment. Every morning, when she walked to her desk, there it was, bringing a smile to her face. When she worked, she could feel him behind her, warm and encouraging. He was abroad at the moment but he would be returning to England the following evening and she would meet him, listen to how his visit to the US had gone and, under normal circumstances, share a meal, exchange news, both of them tacitly deferring the time when words would give way to the inevitable gloriously fulfilling meeting of bodies on his giant-sized bed with which she had become very familiar.

Under normal circumstances.

Her undoing had been to think that what they had qualified as *normal*. She had told herself so many times at the beginning that it was never going to be the sort of relationship that went anywhere, that she should envisage the end before it was staring her in the face, that with a man like Rafe it was all about appreciating the moment and never expecting it to go anywhere.

But the weeks had rolled by and she had settled into a false sense of security. She had learnt never to talk about a future or plan anything at all. That way, when it was over she could at least be mentally prepared, or as mentally prepared as she could be given that with each passing day she had fallen deeper and deeper in love with him.

That was something she kept well hidden from him. There weren't many situations Rafe couldn't handle, but a woman declaring her love ranked up there at the top of the list.

And she didn't want to lose him. Not yet. Not when there was still a tomorrow for them. She would know, she told herself repeatedly, when he was beginning to tire of her. She would be able to sense it and would take the necessary action, make the first move.

Maybe, she occasionally told herself, she wouldn't wait until then. Maybe she would cut it off if only to spare Claudia and Grace the eventual disappointment, because if she had become more and more emotionally wrapped up with him over time, then so too had their aspirations for the fairy-tale ending.

They had visited four times in the space of two months and each time had seen an escalation in their hopes for a white wedding, even though Sophie had laughingly changed the subject every single time her mother had raised it.

But there just never seemed a right time to end it. He would shut that door behind him, switch on the lights in his apartment and she would melt. Her lips would find his, her arms would wind around his neck and her body would yield to his, quivering to his every touch as hotly and crazily as it had done from that very first time.

Fate had a nasty way of making sure that happiness never outstayed its welcome.

She bided her time at the office, doing what she needed to until it was time to go back to her flat, but it wasn't easy.

Worse was the following day. Rafe had sent her a text

just before he left America, one of his sexy text messages that always made her look over her shoulder to make sure that no one was hovering behind her. She was to meet him at his apartment, preferably wearing her birthday suit but, failing that, as little as possible.

The thought of doing any such thing now made her feel sick. She glanced down at her handbag where the end of her dream was burning a hole in the bag. One light, virtually non-existent period five weeks ago, and then nothing at all. She hadn't even twigged at first because they had been scrupulous in their precautions. Her brain had only begun to crank into gear that morning, working out that, yes, there had been that one time, that very first time, when they had used nothing. After they had returned from Cornwall, she had gone to her doctor and had asked for whatever the lowest dosage pill was. So she had gained a slight amount of weight. That, she had read, could be attributed to her contraception, and, besides, hadn't Rafe told her that the few extra pounds added to her sexiness?

Even buying the pregnancy-testing kit hadn't sent her stomach into too much of a panicked overdrive because, really, the fact that her periods had been inconsistent was far more likely to be caused by starting on a new pill.

She had slipped the little device into her handbag and had forgotten all about it. Until a couple of hours ago when her world had come grinding to a halt.

She waited until she was the last in the office and then made her way home. Rafe was expecting her later, much later, ten o'clock. Normally, she would have gone to his apartment earlier, let herself in using the key he had had made for her weeks back, when he had decided that arranging to meet was ridiculous when what he wanted was to get back to his place and find her there, waiting for him.

She might have rifled his fridge for something to eat, then watched television, enjoying the slow uncurling of excitement as the hour of his return got closer.

Instead, she had used the toilet, then walked around her flat for three hours, pausing every fifteen minutes to look at that little stick. Somewhere along the line, she had a bath and changed into jeans and a jumper. She switched on the television for noise, but she couldn't focus, couldn't think of anything but what she would say to Rafe. Tell him? She had to. She didn't live in a vacuum. There was no way that she could run away and hide, or disappear off the face of the earth, and even if she could have she didn't think she could leave without giving him the chance to know that he was going to be a father.

At nine-fifteen, she wearily got a taxi to his house and waited in the sitting room, half praying that he would be late, that she would have time to fall asleep and put off the dreadful moment, half hoping that he showed up early so that she could say what she had to say and get it over with.

She didn't want to dwell on his reaction, but she couldn't avoid it.

Hadn't he made a passing remark once about women who trapped men into marriage by getting pregnant? On the back of some programme they had watched together? She was sure of it. And she had agreed with him!

She was weak with nerves when she finally heard the sound of his key in the door.

She had left the overhead lights off, choosing to switch on the two standing lights instead, all the better to conceal the expression on his face when she broke the news.

She heard his footsteps heading towards the sitting room, imagining him expecting…what? The look of pleasure on her face as she saw him? The parted lips and shining eyes as she welcomed him back? Certainly he wouldn't have expected to find her curled into the chair by the fireplace, legs tucked under her, dressed in the opposite of *as little as possible*.

He paused in the doorway, quickly taking in the scene presented in front of him, then he strolled slowly towards her, thankfully leaving the overhead lights switched off.

When he was standing over her, he smiled, that slow, lazy smile that always sent her senses spinning into orbit, and for the space of a few seconds she was very tempted to enjoy just one last night together before she broke the news.

'I've brought you back something.' He reached into his jacket pocket and extracted a navy blue box, which Sophie dutifully took. A little china pig. She had told him that she collected china pigs and he had laughed at that, but ever since, wherever he went, he always somehow managed to bring her back one to add to her growing collection.

'Thank you,' she said, opening and shutting the box and then sticking it on the table next to her.

'What's wrong?'

'There's something I have to tell you.'

'Should I pour myself a stiff drink first?' But he was still smiling, although there was curiosity in his eyes now.

Several might do the trick, Sophie thought. 'No. Just sit down. My neck's hurting looking up at you.'

He frowned and then dragged a footstool over to her chair and squatted on it. 'What's the matter?'

'First of all, I just want to tell you that I won't be marrying you.' He opened his mouth to say something and Sophie held one hand up to stop him before he could speak. 'I've had fun, Rafe—'

'Had?'

'Please. Don't interrupt. Please.' Her eyes slid away from his. She couldn't bear the intensity of his stare. 'It's important that we get one or two things straight. Well, that I do. We both knew that this wasn't going to last for ever…the only way things last for ever is if two people get married, and I don't want to marry you.' The lie made her mouth taste sour, but it was a lie that had to be told.

'I don't know what the hell has caused this, Sophie—'

'Nothing's *caused* it. Time's caused it.'

'When I spoke to you yesterday you were fine, looking forward to seeing me…'

She could see his mind ticking, trying to work out what was going on, meticulously piecing together the facts at his disposal.

'Something's happened and you're going to tell me what.' He stood up, pushing the stool from under him, and began prowling the room, as if there was too much energy inside him for him to sit still. 'It must be to do with Grace. Or Claudia. Or both. Have they said anything to you? Warned you off me? No, that doesn't make sense. Why would they do that? They've been as happy as little sandboys thinking that we were going out together. Unless one of them has had second thoughts? Is that it?'

'No, Rafe.'

'What, then?' He removed his jacket and pitched it on the sofa so that he could continue his restless prowl, rolling up the sleeves of his shirt in the process. 'Is there someone else?' He stopped dead and stared at her. In the absence of any other scenarios, his brain had seized upon this one and was trying it on for size.

'Rafe…'

'Is there?'

Before she could open her mouth, he had closed the space between them so that he could lean over her, crowding her into the chair.

'No!' She inserted that before he could launch into a

string of accusations about a piece of fiction. 'Of course there isn't anyone else! When would I have time for that?'

'What, then? Why don't you stop beating about the bush and just tell me what the hell is going on here?'

'Rafe, I'm pregnant.'

The three words dropped like a bombshell into still water. She held her breath, waiting for detonation. None came. He turned away from her and walked towards the sofa so that he could sit down. Even then, for a few hideous seconds, he didn't look at her, just stared in front of him, his face wiped clean of any emotion.

Shock, horror, rage…she didn't know what was building up inside him.

'You're pregnant,' he finally said, turning to face her.

'I know it's a shock. I only…well, did the test today, found out…it was that first time…an accident…who would have thought that just that once would have…would have…?' She plucked anxiously at the hem of her jumper, staring down at the tips of her bare toes. She had kicked off her shoes earlier on. 'I never meant for it to happen, Rafe, you have to believe me. Which is why I told you that I wouldn't marry you…'

'Because you're carrying my baby?' He gave a short, dry burst of laughter. 'Funny reason. You don't have a choice, though, Sophie.'

'What do you mean?'

'I mean that no baby of mine will be born illegitimate. I mean that, whether you want to or not, you will marry me.'

'D-don't be silly,' Sophie stammered. Yes, somewhere at the back of her mind, she had faced this possibility, that he would ask her to marry him. She had faced it and had rejected it out of hand because to marry someone for all the wrong reasons was to condemn that marriage to failure.

A few months ago, she would have been distraught at the idea of bringing a baby into the world as a single mother, but he had given her strength and confidence in herself, enough for her to know that, however hard the going was, she would be able to cope on her own. And it would be a damn sight better than to see him trapped in a loveless marriage, blaming her for laying the trap, probably finding pleasure outside and justifying his infidelity because of the situation to which he had been forced to bend. A bird with clipped wings, and she would become the one with the knife in her hands. No! Every bit of her revolted against the prospect.

'No, Rafe, I won't.' She took a deep breath and looked at him steadily. 'A marriage without love is no marriage, and any child growing up with two parents who don't love each other, would end up a very unhappy child. Not to mention how we would fare. No, better for us to part company—and, of course, you would be able to see him or her whenever you wanted. I would never try and stop that.'

'It's out of the question.'

'Don't tell me what I'm going to do!' Sophie burst out. 'You can't drag me up an altar and force me to say *I do*!'

'Try me.' He leant forward, elbows on his thighs and gave her a cool, sideways look. 'I mean it, Sophie. My baby will be born a Loro and he will have all the advantages that come with the name.'

'But what about love?' Sophie cried.

'What about the alternative?'

'What alternative?'

'I can always fight for custody. Has that occurred to you?'

It hadn't, but it was occurring now, and she looked at him in dawning horror until he sighed and stood up.

'I could, but I wouldn't.' He walked over to her and sat

back down on the stool. 'Not every marriage starts with fireworks,' he said heavily, his green eyes settling on her face.

'I know, but they should at least start with…with… You're not the marrying kind, Rafe, and I couldn't live with the responsibility of thinking that I'd tied you down when your heart wanted to be free. And I could never live with you leading an outside life.'

'What makes you think that I would be the one who wanted to be free, and who needed to lead an outside life?'

Sophie felt a flutter of something inside, just a second when her heart skipped a beat, and she told herself not to be foolish and start misinterpreting his question, turning it into something she wanted so desperately to hear.

'Because I know,' she said prosaically.

'*You* might get bored.'

'I might.' Round about the same time as hell froze over. Disillusioned, yes. Hurt, certainly. But bored, never. If boredom was all she had to envisage being married to Rafe, then it would have been a very small price to pay.

'However bored you get, there'll be no looking around. You do realise that, don't you?'

'Separate rules?' She smiled mirthlessly at him. 'Not that it makes a difference, as the situation won't arise.'

'It'll arise.' Rafe got up and walked slowly over to the fireplace, leaning against it and looking down at her. He was still utterly composed, but something else. She couldn't put her finger on it. An uncertainty that she felt, even though it wasn't immediately evident from his expression. But over the weeks she had fine-tuned her ability to read him, even though she couldn't work out what he could be uncertain about.

'But there won't be separate rules,' he said.

Sophie's eyes widened.

'Is it that inconceivable to take in?' Rafe demanded irritably, a dull, dark flush spreading across his cheekbones. 'If I thought that I would need to fool around with other women, then naturally I wouldn't choose to get married.'

'But...' She frowned and tried hard to make the link between the things he was saying. 'What about when you tire of me?' she asked. 'You're not built for permanence. You know that. You've told me that before.'

'Have I? I don't recall.'

'Of course you have, Rafe. It's always been a given.'

'Well, I've told you that I won't be fooling around and you will just have to take my word for it.'

'You're saying that fatherhood is that important to you that you would sacrifice what you wanted to do for the sake of it?'

'A child needs emotional stability,' Rafe said darkly. 'And anyway...'

'Anyway?' There it went again. That little flutter like a message being dangled in front of her that was very nearly legible inside her head, but not quite, a message that would thrill her to the very core.

'Fun can lead to other things, deeper things.'

'What does that mean? You're talking in riddles.'

For a man whose grasp of the English language never failed to astound her, he was certainly having a lot of trouble with it now. Either that or her brain had gone into partial shut-down.

'We've had a good time together, Sophie. Sexually, we're compatible...'

'Which is fine when it's all about sex!'

'You had your chance to speak, now let me speak without interrupting.' He waited a few seconds, as if making sure that the stage was his. 'And we get along. You can't deny that, can you? No, you can't. So don't tell me that we can't make a marriage out of that, and a good marriage, something solid that a child of ours would thrive in. A lot of marriages start out with far less.'

But you would still be trapped, Sophie thought. Sure, to start with, things might be fine. There would be the pregnancy, the excitement of being parents, and then what? Were *liking her* and *getting along* sufficient to fuel a rewarding marriage? It might be solid because they wouldn't be bickering from dawn till dusk, but affection wouldn't be enough. Couldn't he see that? Not for her and certainly not for him. And, whether he wanted to admit it or not, he would eventually want to seek out newer pastures, because unless sex grew into something deeper and more encompassing it withered away. If they were to marry, it would wither away into resentment. And with the best intentions in the world, what red-blooded male would sit back and deal with resentment with a smile on his face?

And she would have the double agony of watching that resentment bloom, knowing that her love was never to be returned.

'Stop shaking your head!' Rafe exploded. 'I am appealing to your sense of logic, but it doesn't matter anyway. We will be married!'

'No!' She stared at him in stormy silence for a second, then took a breath. 'But I understand what you're saying. I know it's important to you that our…our child gets the benefit of both parents…' *Our child.* Whatever kind of mess she was now in, she still felt a bubble of joy at the thought of being pregnant, of carrying the child of the man she loved. He was very still and turned away from her. 'Which is why perhaps there's a compromise…'

Rafe didn't say anything.

'Aren't you going to ask me what?'

'Tell me.'

She wished that he would at least look at her while she spoke, but he didn't. He stared in frowning concentration at the ground, only the inclination of his head indicating that he was waiting to hear what she had to say. It was an idea that hadn't occurred to her before, but now it seemed to make perfect sense.

'You're right. We get along and that's obviously important. So here's my idea: I think we should perhaps think about moving in together.' It felt shamefully brazen to be suggesting cohabitation, but she consoled herself with the fact that he had already proposed marriage, which was a much bigger step, and, really, what she was offering was the best of both worlds. He liked things to make sense and this made sense. 'I mean,' she rushed along, warming to the idea as she was released from the immediate pain of wrenching herself out of their relationship, 'that way we would be both together when the baby's born and it's not as committal as marriage. If at any point you started to have second thoughts, there would be no divorce, no legal wrangles. I would even be happy to sign an agreement, so that you would be safe in the knowledge that I wasn't going to ever consider fleecing you of any of your money...'

'And all this because you don't think that a marriage without love is worth anything?'

'We would make each other unhappy in the long run. I'm just giving you a more reasonable option.'

'And what if there's love on one side?' He looked directly at her although he remained very still.

'What do you mean?'

'It means that I don't want a way out with you.'

Sophie felt the blood rush to her face, and even then she was scared to read the obvious into what he was saying. That he loved her? What else could he mean?

'You don't have to tell lies, Rafe,' she said in a small voice.

'You should know by now that I never feel obliged to do anything.' There was some of the old arrogance there, enough to make her want to smile, because what she had discovered over time was that his arrogance was of a particularly endearing nature. But he was still hesitant and she held her breath, waiting for him to continue and trying to stamp down the wild singing in her head.

He walked over to her and resumed sitting on the stool. Sophie wondered whether she would ever be able to look at that stool again and not remember this evening.

'I don't know when it happened...' He paused and Sophie hoped he wasn't expecting her to interrupt him. Right now she just wanted him to keep on talking. 'I realised early on that I was attracted to you, and I'm ashamed to say that I assumed it was because you were so different from any of the women I had ever dated before.'

'You mean I was a novelty? Like a toy pulled out of a Christmas stocking?' She struggled to feel insulted by this, but couldn't. Not when he was staring at her in ways that were making her melt.

'A rather wonderful toy, as it turned out. A toy that had the ability to turn into a million different things...' He reached out and played with her fingers. 'I started out wanting to sleep with you, then I found that I enjoyed talking to you, hearing what you had to say, and then you began to influence me. You are the reason I did that deal with Bob. You made me think, see things in a different way. I still told myself that really, underneath it all, I was a free man, but you were in my head night and day. When we came down to Cornwall... I jumped at the chance, and when we made love and were in the bedroom and my dearest mama knocked on the door...I made sure that I was the one to open it. I knew exactly what she would think and I wanted it. I didn't look any further than knowing that I didn't want to end what we had, nor did I want it to be something kept under wraps. It was only when I was away for these past three days that it hit me.'

Sophie was riveted.

'I never wanted you out of my life because I wanted you and needed you, and, somewhere along the line, I had fallen in love with you.'

'You've fallen in love with me,' she repeated in wonderment.

'So, you see, I don't want to marry you because you've announced that you're pregnant.' He stood up and walked over to his jacket, and then handed her another box, this one smaller. 'I was planning on giving this to you tonight.'

Sophie's fingers were trembling as she opened the box and there it was. A ring. Small, sleek, with three diamonds set in a line at the top. The most wonderful thing she had ever seen.

She looked at him and flung her arms around his neck. 'Yes! Yes, yes, yes!'

'You accept, then?'

'Rafe, I love you. I've loved you for ages. I just never thought…never imagined that you could ever return my love and I so wanted you not to feel trapped into marrying me because you felt you had to…' She drew back and tenderly traced the lines of his beautiful face. 'I can't think that there's anyone else in the world happier than me at this moment.'

'My darling,' he murmured, capturing one hand in his and kissing her lightly on the mouth. 'I will do my utmost to ensure that there never will be.'

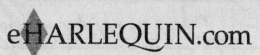

If you enjoyed what you just read,
then we've got an offer you can't resist!

Take 2 bestselling love stories FREE!

Plus get a FREE surprise gift!

Clip this page and mail it to Harlequin Reader Service®

IN U.S.A.	IN CANADA
3010 Walden Ave.	P.O. Box 609
P.O. Box 1867	Fort Erie, Ontario
Buffalo, N.Y. 14240-1867	L2A 5X3

YES! Please send me 2 free Harlequin Presents® novels and my free surprise gift. After receiving them, if I don't wish to receive anymore, I can return the shipping statement marked cancel. If I don't cancel, I will receive 6 brand-new novels every month, before they're available in stores! In the U.S.A., bill me at the bargain price of $3.80 plus 25¢ shipping & handling per book and applicable sales tax, if any*. In Canada, bill me at the bargain price of $4.47 plus 25¢ shipping & handling per book and applicable taxes**. That's the complete price and a savings of at least 10% off the cover prices—what a great deal! I understand that accepting the 2 free books and gift places me under no obligation ever to buy any books. I can always return a shipment and cancel at any time. Even if I never buy another book from Harlequin, the 2 free books and gift are mine to keep forever.

106 HDN DZ7Y
306 HDN DZ7Z

_____

Name   (PLEASE PRINT)

_____

Address   Apt.#

_____

City   State/Prov.   Zip/Postal Code

Not valid to current Harlequin Presents® subscribers.

Want to try two free books from another series?
Call 1-800-873-8635 or visit www.morefreebooks.com.

* Terms and prices subject to change without notice. Sales tax applicable in N.Y.
** Canadian residents will be charged applicable provincial taxes and GST.
All orders subject to approval. Offer limited to one per household.
® are registered trademarks owned and used by the trademark owner and or its licensee.

PRES04R   ©2004 Harlequin Enterprises Limited